Kicked out . . .

"Molly," Ms. Thacker said calmly, "Mr. Thacker and I have been discussing you at great length, as you may imagine."

Molly sat in the school office, facing the Thackers. It was almost dinnertime, and Molly was worn out from the hard day she'd had. She was very hungry.

"I kept you here after your father's death out of the goodness of my heart," Ms. Thacker said. "But you have proven remarkably ungrateful. You defy my wishes and ignore your studies, and now it seems you are inciting others to defy me also." Ms. Thacker's steely eyes bored into Molly's.

"Therefore, Mr. Thacker and I have decided that you may remain at Glenmore until the end of the school year. At that time we will relinquish our custody of you, and you will be put into foster care."

Don't miss the other books in this
heartwarming new series:

Princess

Princess

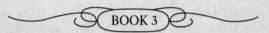 BOOK 3

Home at Last

GABRIELLE CHARBONNET

AN
APPLE
PAPERBACK

SCHOLASTIC INC.
New York Toronto London Auckland Sydney

ISBN 0-590-22289-9

Produced by Daniel Weiss Associates, Inc.,
33 West 17th Street, New York, NY 10011.

12 11 10 9 8 7 6 5 4 3 2 1   5 6 7 8 9/9 0/0

Printed in the U.S.A.   40

First Scholastic printing, July 1995

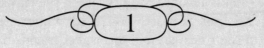

1

The Great Escape

This is it. There's no turning back now, Molly thought as she let herself out of the servants' door of Glenmore Academy. She was standing in a narrow alley. The first pink rays of dawn were struggling to break through the heavy snow clouds that had covered Boston for the past few days. Even in the alley, sandwiched tightly between Glenmore and the stone townhouse next door, several inches of dry, crunchy snow covered the ground.

Molly hitched her pillowcase higher on her shoulder. She hadn't had many possessions to pack, and the pillowcase wasn't heavy. By the time she emerged onto the street in back of Glenmore, light snowflakes were already falling again.

Good-bye, Glenmore, Molly thought. *Good-bye, Lucy. Good-bye, Evie.* She didn't mind leaving the exclusive boarding school that had been her home for the last six months. But leaving Lucy Axminster and Evie Lucas was much harder. They were her best friends—her only friends. They had stuck by her when she went from riches to rags, from privileged star pupil to pathetic charity case. Ever since Molly's father, the famous film-maker Michael Stewart, had died while making a movie in the Brazilian rain forest, her friends had been the only thing keeping her going.

Molly walked past the townhouse next door, automatically glancing up at its windows to see if she could catch sight of Mr. Tibbs. When Glenmore's headmistress, Cathy Thacker, had made Molly get rid of her beloved kitten, Molly had found him a new home next door. A kind-looking lady lived there, and she had a young assistant Molly had spoken to once. They were taking care of Mr. Tibbs now. Sometimes Molly could actually see him sitting in a window, looking plush and well fed. She was so thankful for those rare glimpses.

But on this cold mid-March morning, the windows were dark and there was no sign of the fuzzy, blue-gray kitten who had helped Molly through her first lonely weeks at Glenmore. Well, it was still very early. She was escaping before Ms. Thacker could send her out on errands. It was a new morning, and now Molly was free.

Two blocks away from the school was a trolley stop, and a trolley was pulling up. Molly ran to jump on board, searching in her pockets for money to pay the fare. Beyond sneaking out of school, she hadn't really planned where to go. Riding in a warm trolley for a while would give her time to think.

Inside the almost-empty car, Molly leaned her head against the window and tried to make some kind of plan. The night before, things had seemed so hopeless, her problems so unsolvable. Then she had come up with the idea of running away. Somehow, she thought—she didn't know how—it would make her life better. Now here she was on her own, heading away from Glenmore. But she hadn't slept well, and it was so early in the morning . . . before she knew it, the rhythmic clicking of the trolley's wheels had lulled her into an uneasy sleep.

"Where was she going?" Leslie Banks asked her assistant, Toby Daniels.

Toby shrugged helplessly. "I don't know. I just assumed she was on one of her weird errands. You know how she seems to come and go at all hours of the day."

In the stone townhouse next to Glenmore, Leslie Banks paced up and down. She had rented the house in Boston in order to work on her latest project: a documentary about the struggle between the native people and the government in the Brazilian rain forest. One of her most gifted former students had begun the film last fall. Just after she had arrived in Brazil to help him begin the preliminary editing, he had died of a tropical disease. Now she was trying to finish his work alone.

Leslie threw up her hands. "Why am I even thinking about her? I have my hands full with the movie, and with looking for *another* little girl."

As her friend had lain dying in his canvas tent, surrounded by the overgrown, steamy jungle, Leslie had sat next to him on the floor. Blinking back her tears, she'd bathed his face with cool water and murmured comforting words. But they had both known he wasn't going to make it.

Just before he closed his eyes for the last time, he had gripped Leslie's hand. "My daughter . . ." he had gasped.

"Yes, Michael, I know. What about her?" Leslie had whispered.

"Take care of her," came the weak response. "You take care of her. . . . No one else." Then his eyelids had fluttered shut, his breathing had become more labored, and Leslie had known it was the end.

So Leslie had found herself suddenly expected to care for a child she hadn't seen in nine years. Out of love and respect for her old friend, she decided to do it, to take care of Michael's daughter as if she were her own. There was only one problem: Leslie had no idea where to find her. It was making her frantic.

"I know," Toby said now. "But I keep thinking about that little girl from the school. She's always running around the neighborhood, lugging packages, looking thin and unhappy." He paused for a moment, looking at his boss. "There's just something about her, her life, that interests me. When I saw her leaving so early this morning, with a pillowcase over her shoulder, it just seemed weird, that's all." The young man pushed his black hair out of his eyes. "It was barely dawn."

"Do you think she was stealing something from the school?" Leslie frowned, trying to put her own lost little girl out of her mind.

Toby shrugged again. "Anyway, there's no point thinking about it. I don't know where she went. I'd better get some work done now if I'm going to the train station later to pick up all that film stock you ordered."

"Okay. Let me know if you see the blond kid again. It does seem strange for her to be out wandering around so early. I wonder if her parents know what she does at that school."

Evie Lucas looked at the clock, then faced Ms. Thacker again. "I don't know where Molly is," she said, a touch of defiance in her voice. "She wasn't at breakfast."

The headmistress's pale, pretty face tightened with anger. "I hope she doesn't think that because it's Saturday she doesn't have any responsibilities," she said, a thread of tension in her voice. "Go up to her room and tell her that if she isn't in my office in five minutes flat, she'll be very sorry."

Somehow Evie resisted the urge to salute Ms. Thacker and click her heels together. Once she was out of the school office, Evie ran down the main hall and into the girls' dorm. The elevator took her to the fourth floor, then she climbed the steps to the fifth-floor attic, where she and Molly, as charity students, had their rooms.

When Molly hadn't shown up that morning to help Evie sort newspapers, one of their many work-study jobs, Evie hadn't worried. She'd hoped Molly was sleeping late.

Now Evie opened Molly's door, praying that Molly wasn't sick or something, and that somehow she could get downstairs in five minutes.

The room was empty. Evie ran across the hall and checked the bathroom. Empty. Back in Molly's room she saw the naked pillow without its case. She opened the closet. Some clothes were missing. Molly's hiding place for her journal was empty, too. There was a small piece of board missing from the back of the closet, making a hole that led into the back of Evie's closet next door. They used this small window to communicate when they were being punished and weren't allowed to talk to each other. Now Evie saw a piece of folded white paper stuck in the open gap.

There were two notes, one addressed to her, one to Lucy. Evie stuck Lucy's note into her pocket, then quickly unfolded her own.

Dear Evie,
    By the time you read this
I'll be gone. I can't take
Glenmore and Ms. Thacker

6

anymore. She hates me, and she'll make my life horrible no matter what I do. I don't know where I'm going, but I wish you could come with me. I'll miss you and Lucy so much, all the time.

I hope things with your mom go okay. Someday I'll come back and find you, and then we can have our bakery together.

Love always,
Molly

P.S. Thank you for being my friend.

Evie sat down on the floor of the closet, stunned. Molly had run away! She'd never even hinted that she was thinking about it. Evie had no idea what to do. Should she tell Ms. Thacker? The headmistress would be furious. On the other hand, it wasn't safe for Molly to be wandering the streets of Boston alone. Should she call the police? She wanted Molly to be happy, and she knew Molly was right about Ms. Thacker making her miserable. But how could Molly take care of herself? She was only eleven years old.

Evie had to go downstairs. She had to tell Ms. Thacker something. But what?

Molly came awake with a jolt. She was in a trolley car by herself. The trolley was standing still. Sitting up, she peered through the window. They were at the end of the line, out in the suburbs away from Boston. There was a platform where people were waiting, but the doors were closed. Molly had a moment of panic. Would she be trapped here? She wouldn't have to spend the night alone in the trolley barn, would she?

Then the doors whooshed open, and several people got on and took their seats. Some of them looked at Molly curiously. A few minutes later the car started down the tracks in the opposite direction, heading back to town. Molly felt both relieved and worried. What was she going to do now? She was running away, but where was she running *to*? If only she were older—she could get a job somewhere, save her money, move to another city. But she was only eleven.

The ride back to Boston took almost an hour. A light snow was falling, but inside the trolley it was warm and comfortable. When Molly noticed they were close to Glenmore's neighborhood, she sank down in her seat and looked over the edge of her window. But she didn't see signs that anyone was looking for her, not on the trolley line, at least.

They passed Glenmore's stop and continued

downtown. Molly had never taken the trolley in this direction before, so she eagerly watched the passing scenery. Her car was very crowded now. No one seemed to think it was strange that a little girl was traveling by herself on a Saturday morning. Molly grinned—she was blending in.

The buildings outside the windows got taller and closer together. One of them caught Molly's attention. It was a large gray building with wide steps. It looked like a courthouse or something, but its sign said BOSTON PUBLIC LIBRARY. Instantly Molly stood up and pulled the cord to signal a stop. She got off the trolley and headed for the library, her worn-out sneakers crunching through the powdery snow that was a couple of inches thick on the ground.

Soon Molly was up the stairs and pushing open the huge, heavy brass doors of the library. The children's section was on the third floor. Inside the library it was peaceful and quiet, and it felt like a haven. Molly found a book by an author she liked and settled down by a window. Until she had some idea of where she was going and what she was going to do, it would be best to stay there. It wasn't much of a plan, but it was a start.

"She did what?" Lucy Axminster's blue eyes were round behind her gold wire-rimmed glasses.

"Shh." Evie motioned with her hand, and she and Lucy hunkered down over their lunch trays. "Molly ran away. Here's a note she wrote to you. I've been looking for you all morning." She slipped the folded piece of paper to Lucy.

So far that morning Evie had managed to elude Ms. Thacker, but she knew time was running out. Maybe if she and Lucy put their heads together, they could come up with some answers.

Lucy carefully read her note under the table, then shoved it in her pocket. Her eyes looked shiny. "I can't believe she didn't talk to us about this," she whispered. "She knows she can trust us. Why didn't she say something?"

"I don't know." Evie shrugged. "But we have to figure out how to help her. It was stupid of her to run away," she whispered angrily. "It's too danger-ous. Molly might know how to order food in French at some fancy restaurant, but there's no way she can take care of herself on the street. We have to do something—for her own good."

"But what?" Lucy pushed her food around with a fork. "If we tell the Thwacker, she'll go ballistic. Maybe we should try to look for her ourselves."

Evie snorted. "Oh, yeah. *That's* practical. Let's just go comb the city of Boston. That shouldn't take more than, like, six months."

"Then *what*?" Lucy's eyes flashed.

"I think we need to tell someone," Evie said slowly. "But who?"

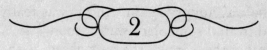

2

Nowhere to Run

At lunchtime Molly spent a dollar fifty on a hot dog from a street vendor. That left her with only two dollars to her name. After lunch she walked around downtown, trying to come up with a course of action. *Could I just hide forever in the library?* she wondered. *It's so big, and there are bathrooms. But how would I eat?* It was pretty cold, and the tall downtown buildings created wind tunnels that whipped the cold breeze into a stiff, freezing wall of air. Soon Molly's nose was numb, and so were her feet. Her pillowcase started to feel heavy.

Maybe I could hide in a department store, she thought, pausing to look in a store window. *One that has a lunch counter. That would take care of food. I could sleep in the mattress department.* She almost grinned at the thought, rubbing her hands together and stamping her feet to stay warm.

Could I hitchhike south? The idea seemed too scary. She looked up at the sky. It was already midafternoon. It would be getting dark in another hour or so. The hot dog hadn't really filled her up—she was hungry again. And it was really cold; she had to find someplace warm, soon.

Turning the corner, she was faced with a big building that she recognized. The train station! It was where all the subway lines came together, and all the commuter trains too. It was big, and well lit, and full of people. She would be warm and unnoticed and safe there. Hitching up her pillowcase again, she hurried across the wide avenue.

"Girls, I'm afraid we have to call the police," Jerry Thacker said in his soft voice. "We have to do what's best for Molly."

Evie and Lucy looked at the ground. Lucy felt scared. She couldn't believe it had come to this. The thought of Molly wandering the streets of Boston, alone, in winter, made Lucy's throat feel tight. After much discussion, Lucy and Evie had decided to tell the headmaster, Mr. Thacker. They hardly ever dealt with him, since he ran the boys' section of Glenmore, and his wife, Cathy, ran the girls'. But everyone knew he was much nicer than Ms. Thacker.

"Now, is there anything at all you can think of that you should tell me? Anywhere Molly ever mentioned she wanted to go?"

Lucy felt confused. Molly had lived all over the world, traveling with her famous father on location.

"She liked Taiwan a lot," she said hesitantly.

A faint smile crossed Mr. Thacker's bland face. "I meant in Boston. I think we can rule out Taiwan for now."

Lucy and Evie shook their heads.

Then Evie said, "She liked Faneuil Hall, for shopping. And she liked the stables—Pink's and Lytton's. Where she used to have her pony."

Until you and Ms. Thacker sold him to Celeste Foucher, Lucy thought bitterly.

"Okay," Mr. Thacker said. "Thank you. I'll call the police now, and let them know she's missing."

"Who's missing?"

Lucy winced at the headmistress's voice. This was just what she and Evie had been trying to avoid. Ms. Thacker could be very nasty when things didn't go her way.

Mr. Thacker looked up. "It's Molly Stewart, dear. She seems to have run away."

The headmistress went pale, making her dark eyes stand out. "What?" she exclaimed.

"Now, let's just remain calm," Mr. Thacker said soothingly. "I'm going to call the police, and I'm sure she'll turn up in no time."

Ms. Thacker whirled on Lucy and Evie. "What do you know about this?" she demanded. "What did she tell you?"

"Nothing," Evie said defiantly, crossing her arms over her chest. "She didn't tell us anything."

13

"You're lying!" Ms. Thacker cried. "I'll punish you! I'll punish both of you! Now tell me where she is. The last thing we need is some spoiled, stuck-up princess going around telling lies about this school."

Lucy stared at her in disbelief. She had no idea what Ms. Thacker was talking about. What did she think Molly was doing?

"We don't know where she is," Lucy repeated impatiently. Until now her rule had always been to stay out of Ms. Thacker's way and not get into trouble. But anger was overcoming her natural reserve. "And you can't punish us for not knowing anything."

Ms. Thacker's small white hands clenched at her sides. "Oh? We'll see about that. I know you helped her. I know you know something."

"Dear, please calm down," Mr. Thacker said firmly.

Ms. Thacker stared at him as if he had just sprouted two heads.

"I'm calling the police now, and we need to be calm," he pointed out.

Lucy watched the headmistress take several deep breaths.

"I'm not finished with you two yet," Ms. Thacker promised. "You *will* be punished."

"I don't think my parents would be very happy about that," Lucy said pointedly. *Of course, right now they're in the middle of getting divorced, and they barely know I'm alive, but* she *doesn't need to know that.*

"The Dukes wouldn't like it, either," Evie said

coldly. Melina Duke was an alumna of Glenmore, and she and her husband were Evie's patrons, because Evie was a charity student. Evie had recently gone to visit them at their New Hampshire home, and now she felt they were her friends.

"Get out," Ms. Thacker said, her voice shaking. "I'll deal with you two later."

In the hall outside the school office, Lucy leaned against the wall. She felt all shaken up: worried, angry, disgusted. Mostly worried.

"Oh, Evie," she breathed. "Do you think we did the right thing?"

"I don't know." Evie punched the upholstered chair next to her. "I really don't know."

"Come in, Mr. Price," Leslie Banks said, waving him into her study. "I hope you have good news for me."

The private investigator sank down into a leather armchair and brushed some snow off his hat. "I'm sorry, Ms. Banks," he said. "I've traced Michael Stewart and his daughter as far as Nantucket, where they were at the end of last summer, but no further. If I could only get a couple of his credit card receipts, at least I would know what city to look in. What country. But all his financial records have been seized by the IRS until they decide what to do with what's left of his estate. Frankly, it's amazing that *anything* is left—Michael Stewart's lawyers seemed to think his entire fortune had been completely lost."

Sighing heavily, Leslie flopped down onto the sofa. The weight of disappointment bent her shoulders forward. She rubbed her hands across her eyes. "Look," she said wearily, brushing a few strands of hair off her face, "I know he put her in a boarding school somewhere—he mentioned it on the phone, before I went out there. He said . . ." Leslie's voice choked up as she remembered one of the last conversations she'd had with her good friend. "He said the separation was killing him. It looks like he was right."

Richard Price waited in respectful silence. He'd always been a big fan of Michael Stewart's films, and the news of his unexpected death had been a shame. It was a privilege to look for the filmmaker's missing daughter, but so far she had been impossible to trace.

"What I'm saying is," Leslie continued more calmly, "there can't be that many boarding schools in the United States. Surely a simple phone call to each of them. . . . We have to find her. We just have to. I promised Michael, before he died."

"I understand your frustration," Mr. Price said. "But there are literally hundreds of boarding schools in the country—and most of them won't give out information about their students. Parents, especially famous ones, pay a lot for confidentiality. And after we get through with all the schools in the United States, there's the rest of North America, and Europe, to consider. It's also possible he sent her back to school in Taiwan. And even if we find the school she was in, there's no guarantee she'll still be there. If no one was paying the bill—"

"Mr. Price!" Leslie sat up straight and angrily tugged on her sweater sleeves. "I've hired you to find the answers. I don't care how much it costs. I want every one of those schools contacted. I want you to explore other avenues—the foster care system, for instance. It's your job to turn over every stone and look behind every door. Molly Stewart must be found. Who's taking care of her now? How is she living? She had no relatives—she could be in serious trouble. I must find her. I have to know that she's all right. Am I making myself clear?"

"Yes, Ms. Banks," Mr. Price said sympathetically. "I'll do my best. I'll start with the more famous schools—maybe the ones in California, since that's where a lot of the film industry is. I'll call you with my progress."

"Very good. Thank you, Mr. Price."

Inside the train station it was crowded and busy. It wasn't a very nice train station, Molly thought. Not like Grand Central in Manhattan. It was smaller, less majestic. Little stores selling doughnuts and newspapers and shoeshines and hot dogs lined the big central space. In the middle were a bunch of places to wait for different trains.

Molly walked around, wondering if she should spend the last bit of her money on another hot dog.

17

She took a long drink of water at a water fountain, and went to the bathroom. The bathroom was really yucky, and there was a homeless woman with a shopping cart full of filthy grocery bags. She was washing at one of the sinks. Molly felt sorry for her. *I'm homeless, too,* she thought.

She left the bathroom and found an empty bench to sit on, thinking about the homeless woman. There were lots of homeless people in the train station. Some of them were begging, or were singing for money. Some of them just sat huddled by their small piles of belongings, looking tired or spacey or beaten down.

I'm homeless, too, Molly thought again, *but not like them. If I had to, I could go back to Glenmore.* The very thought made tears well up in her eyes. But seeing all the *really* homeless people made Molly realize that as horrible as Glenmore was, as hateful as Ms. Thacker was, at least Molly could eat good food there. At least when she was in her freezing, depressing little room, she felt safe. She'd bet that these people would be thrilled to trade places with her.

Molly sniffled and wiped her eyes on her jacket sleeve. What was she going to do? She'd sworn not to go back to Glenmore, ever. If she *did* go back, she would be put in solitary confinement for the rest of her life. Ms. Thacker would be twice as mean. What could she do? She sniffled again.

"Are you lost, little girl?" A handsome young man was leaning over her, one foot up on her bench. He smiled, showing lots of teeth. "You look kind of lost. Do you want to talk about it? I'm a good listener."

Instinctively, Molly didn't trust him. "I'm not lost," she said firmly. "I'm waiting for my father."

"Your father, huh?" The young man made a show of looking around. "Where is this father of yours? Where's your mother?"

Molly didn't know what to say. She didn't have a mother. She'd never had one—her mother had died when she was very young. And her father was gone, too. A short distance away, by the doughnut shop, a couple of policemen were talking and drinking coffee. Molly wanted to dash over to them, but she was a runaway. They would make her go back to Glenmore for sure.

"Huh, little girl? Where's your father?" The young man sat down on the bench next to her. "You know what I bet?" he said conversationally. "I bet you're not waiting for your father. Look, it can be tough out here. You're going to need friends. I'm a nice guy. Let's talk about it. Maybe I can help." He was still smiling at her.

Molly didn't say anything. She felt scared and trapped, even though she was in a big, bustling train station, surrounded by people. She had heard about guys like this one. Terrible things happened to kids who trusted strangers.

"Look, are you hungry?" the young man asked. "Why don't you come with me and I'll get you something to eat. You can pay me back later."

That did it. Molly jumped up, grabbed her pillowcase, and took off. Without turning to see if he was following her, she ran across the station and leaped on the first escalator she saw. She ran up the stairs as fast as she could, dodging commuters on their way home from work.

Just ahead were the doors to the street. It was dark outside, but at least it had stopped snowing. Molly ran for the doors, feeling she had to get outside, had to breathe some fresh, cold air.

Wham! Molly blinked and found herself sprawled on the dirty tile floor of the terminal. Large gray metal containers were sliding onto the floor around her, making metallic crashing sounds as they hit. Her pillowcase was thrown several feet away, and a pair of jeans spilled out of it. A tall young man with black hair was desperately grabbing more metal containers that were piled in a stack close by. He was swearing softly under his breath.

Molly realized she must have run smack into him and his film canisters. Looking up, she saw that no one was stopping to help either her or the young man. Everyone was just hurrying by. The gray metal canisters looked so familiar—how many times had she seen her father's film crews lugging them around, shipping them, sorting them, ordering more? It seemed like the last straw; horrified, Molly felt hot tears rolling down her cheeks.

She scrambled to her feet and stuffed her jeans back into the pillowcase.

"Are you okay?" the young man said impatiently, coming over to her. He leaned down and scooped up another film canister. "I guess you didn't see me, huh?" He brushed his black bangs out of his eyes, and his irritated expression cleared. "Hey—it's the little girl from Glenmore!" He gave her a big smile.

Numb, Molly could only stare at him. Then she recognized him, too. It was the young guy who had spoken to her from the skylight across the way. "You live in the townhouse, next to school," she said. "With the lady."

"Just work there," he clarified cheerfully. "The lady's my boss. Listen, are you okay? You kind of barreled into me here."

"I'm sorry," Molly said. "I was just running, and didn't look where I was going."

The young man began stacking his film canisters on their little cart. "You know, I saw you this morning. Where were you going so early?"

Again Molly just stared at him. "You saw me? Did you tell anyone?"

He looked at her curiously. "Just my boss. I thought it was weird, that's all." He grinned. "What were you doing, running away?"

Shocked, Molly turned away, alternately blushing and going pale. That morning she had set off with such high hopes, feeling so free and daring. *Now look at me,* she thought. *I'm hungry, scared, panicking.*

The young man frowned at Molly's reaction. "Were you really running away?" he asked gently.

Another hated tear rolled down her face, and she quickly brushed it away.

"Are you taking a train somewhere?" His voice was kind.

She shook her head. "I don't know where I'm going," she said, her voice cracking. "I don't know what I'm doing." It was a relief to admit it, but she felt strange confiding in a grown-up.

"My name is Toby, Toby Daniels," the young man said. "What's yours?"

Molly felt a moment of fear. Toby seemed like a nice guy, and he was probably helping to take care of Mr. Tibbs, but something inside Molly still felt afraid.

"Anne," she said in a small voice. She blushed at the lie, but he didn't seem to notice.

"Hi, Anne," Toby said warmly. "Look, you know me, I work right next door to your school. Let me buy you a hot chocolate."

This offer felt very different from the stranger's offer just a few minutes before, and Molly decided it would be okay. Soon they were seated at a counter with mugs of steaming hot chocolate before them. To Molly's relief, Toby didn't ask any more questions for a while.

When Molly finished her drink, she felt better, but still exhausted and confused.

"I have to get this stuff to the office," Toby said, leaving money on the counter for a tip. "I'm going to take a taxi. Why don't I give you a ride home?"

Molly could only nod. Her adventure, her chance for freedom, was over. It was time to admit defeat.

They were silent in the taxi during the short ride back to Glenmore. Molly could tell that Toby wanted to ask her all sorts of questions, but she sat far away from him, clutching her pillowcase and staring out the window. The rest of this day was going to be very hard. She only hoped that Toby didn't betray her—didn't tell Ms. Thacker where he'd found her or what she'd been doing. He might, though. Grown-ups always seemed to stick together.

Finally they pulled up in front of Glenmore's impressive stone entrance. Molly waited while Toby unloaded his cargo and paid the driver.

Pulling his cart behind him, he walked her to the wide wooden doors of school.

"Thank you very much for the ride home," Molly said stiffly. "And for the hot chocolate."

"No prob, Anne," Toby said easily. "Listen—" He seemed to hesitate. "If you ever need . . . anything . . . well, we're right next door. My boss is real nice and all."

"Thanks," Molly said, and she gave him a little

smile. Then, her hand shaking, she rang Glenmore's doorbell.

To her amazement, a police officer opened the door. Right behind him was Ms. Thacker. An expression of relief crossed her pretty face, then was immediately replaced by a look of anger.

"You!" she said. "Do you have any idea what trouble you've caused? I don't have time for this nonsense! You're going to be severely punished!"

"Um, excuse me," Toby said from the sidewalk. Both Molly and Ms. Thacker looked at him in surprise.

"She's had a hard day. You might want to go easy on her," Toby said to Ms. Thacker. She just stared at him wordlessly.

Molly pushed open the door and went inside, pausing to give Toby one last timid smile. He gave her a thumbs-up sign, then turned his cart and began to head next door to the townhouse.

Ms. Thacker's angry words and the police officer's questioning passed over Molly's head for a few moments. Toby had actually tried to defend her. He hadn't ratted on her to Ms. Thacker. *I have a new friend,* she thought with amazement. *I have a new friend.*

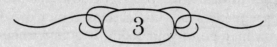

3

Parents' Weekend

Molly followed Ms. Thacker into the school office. She was dimly aware of Mr. Thacker apologizing to the police officer and letting him out the front door. Several students had gathered curiously in the front hall, and the headmaster shooed them away as he closed the office door.

"Molly, dear," he said, "we're so glad to see you safe and sound. We were all so worried about you."

"I'm sorry," Molly said tiredly, knowing her words were inadequate.

"What in the world did you think you were doing?" Ms. Thacker exclaimed. She was frowning, and lines of worry marred her smooth forehead. Nervously she smoothed the skirt of her chic designer suit. "Did you really think you could get away with this stunt?"

Molly had no answer. She was suddenly very weary, and wanted only to go up to her attic room and go to sleep, although it was barely dinnertime.

25

Throwing up her hands, Ms. Thacker said, "I'm too upset to deal with you right now. We'll discuss the consequences of your actions tomorrow. Right now you may go to your room. It goes without saying that you aren't to speak to anyone or take any detours."

Molly nodded without looking at Ms. Thacker. She scooped up her pillowcase, which was now filthy and damp, and left the school office. When she got up to her small, dank room in the fifth-floor attic, she gave it a good look. Was it only this morning she had left it? She felt as if she had been gone for years.

Without warning, her door burst open, and Molly whirled, ready to do battle if Ms. Thacker had changed her mind.

But it was Evie, and she ran to Molly and put her arms around her. Molly was so glad to see her.

"Oh, Molly, forgive us," Evie cried, holding Molly tight. "We were so scared, we didn't know what to do."

Molly hugged her back. "What are you talking about?"

Pulling back, Evie said in a small voice, "We told Mr. Thacker you were gone. Me and Lucy. We were so worried, Mol. I'm really sorry."

"It's okay," Molly said, sinking onto her hard bed. A bedspring poked her in the behind and she said, "Ouch." Then she shook her head. "Of course they would have realized I'd run away. It was a stupid thing to do."

"I know how you feel, Mol," Evie said softly, sitting beside her. "I've been in places where I wanted to run away, too. But it's just too dangerous out there for a kid. Please say you'll try to deal with being here. Me and Lucy were so worried about you all day. I thought . . . I thought . . ." Evie's voice suddenly choked, and she looked away. "Promise you won't run away again—at least not without telling me or Lucy. Okay?"

"Okay," Molly promised. After the day she'd had, it wasn't a hard promise to make. Then the girls heard the heavy footsteps of the older housekeeper, Mary. She acted as a spy for Ms. Thacker and constantly gave Molly and Evie a hard time.

With a rushed "Talk to you later!" Evie slipped out the door and down the hall to her own room just in time.

Mary's footsteps went into the bathroom across the hall. With a sigh, Molly dumped out her pillowcase and put her meager belongings away. She hid her journal in its secret place in the closet. Later she'd have to write in it, all about the day she'd had. But just then all she wanted to do was sleep.

On Monday morning Ms. Thacker put Molly into solitary confinement again. "I feel that mere solitary confinement will have absolutely no effect on you," the headmistress said evenly, brushing some of her dark shiny hair away from her face. "But, frankly, I haven't yet decided what my final course of action should be. In the meantime, solitary will give you time to think over your actions. Of course, I expect you to maintain your usual work-study duties."

"I understand." Molly looked straight ahead, refusing to meet the headmistress's eyes. In truth, she felt so depressed by her adventure that it was a relief to have an excuse not to talk to people. And somehow, everyone seemed to know that she had tried to run away. Molly hated seeing the curiosity in their eyes.

That morning in social studies class Molly tried hard to act as though nothing had happened. But she felt different inside: a little bit colder, more hopeless. She could feel people looking at her, and some kids were whispering. At least her friend Casey Smithers gave her a big smile and lightly punched her shoulder as he walked to his desk. Molly smiled back.

After class Molly bundled up her books and joined the swarm of students hurrying to eat lunch. She herself would eat in the kitchen, alone—fortunately neither Evie nor Lucy had been punished in the end. But Molly would miss seeing them at mealtimes.

"It was really stupid to run away," came a familiar voice at Molly's shoulder.

She turned to see Shannon O'Torr standing beside her. Shannon had changed her hairstyle—now she wore her hair the same way as Leigh Jefferson, one of her new friends.

Molly sighed. Shannon had gone from being one of her good friends to being a complete stranger, and Molly couldn't think of anything to say to her.

"Is it really so bad for you here?" Shannon asked in a low voice.

Turning again to look at her, Molly thought she saw a hint of their old friendship in Shannon's eyes. But when Molly had needed her most, Shannon had deserted her.

"What do you think?" Molly responded, then pressed past Shannon without waiting for a reply.

Dear Journal,
My week of solitary confinement is almost over, but I know things won't get better. Ms. Thacker just says anything she wants to me now, and doesn't care if anyone overhears. Yesterday, after I had been working hard, she said, "Go brush your hair. It looks like

straw." Two eighth graders heard her, and they giggled. It made me so mad. Sometimes I see her looking at me like she's thinking about something. Probably planning what to do to me next.

I've decided to turn my journal into a real book about my life. Maybe years from now it'll be published, and then everyone will know how awful Ms. Thacker was to me. I'm going to write about Evie and Lucy, too.

A light tap on the door made Molly look up. She hoped it wasn't Mary coming to bug her about lights out or something. But when her door opened, Lucy and Evie slipped inside. Without speaking, Evie pushed Molly's towel into the crack under the door so the light wouldn't give them away.

Molly smiled happily. She'd hardly had a chance to talk to either of her friends all week, though of course she and Evie did whisper through their little hole in the closet.

Evie listened for a moment at the door, then nodded and gave her friends a thumbs-up. "I think Mary's down in the employees' lounge, watching TV," she said softly, sitting on Molly's bed.

Lucy and Molly joined her there, and they all sat cross-legged on top of the threadbare blanket.

"It's so cold up here," Lucy complained, rubbing her arms.

Molly chuckled. "After what it's been like most of the winter, this feels positively toasty."

Evie nodded her agreement. "We just wanted to come visit," she said to Molly. "I couldn't wait till Monday, when we could eat together again."

"Ta-daaa," Lucy sang quietly, pulling some sodas and candy from beneath her wool sweater. The three friends fell on the food excitedly.

"So, parents' weekend is coming up," Lucy said after they had finished their candy bars.

Molly nodded, feeling a pang inside. Last fall, she and her dad had eagerly discussed whether or not he would be able to make it. "Do most parents come?" she asked.

"Yeah," Lucy said. "They're really supposed to. It's when they have parent-teacher conferences and all, and they decide whether you can come back next year."

"You mean it isn't just automatic?" Evie asked.

"Uh-uh. There's a huge waiting list to get into Glenmore. If your kid is being a pain, or flunking everything, they just kick him out, no matter how rich you are."

31

"Jeez," Evie said, taking a sip of her soda. "Are your folks coming?"

Lucy frowned. "They came last year. I guess they're going to come this year, too, if they can stop fighting long enough. They kind of have to. I mean, even if they're in the middle of a divorce, they're both still my parents. They have to act like it, right? What about your mom or your grandmother, Evie?"

Evie shook her head fiercely. "No way. I didn't even tell them about it."

"You don't want them to see where you go to school?" Molly asked. It was hard listening to people talk about their parents so casually when she didn't have anyone herself, but she tried not to show her feelings. There wasn't any point in bringing her friends down, too.

"Not really." Evie shrugged. "Besides, you know, they're really busy. Did I tell you my mom got a job?"

"No! That's great," Lucy said. "Where is she working?"

"She got a job as a secretary to a lawyer. She started on Monday. She said she really likes it." Evie tried to sound casual.

"That's fabulous, Evie," Molly said warmly.

"Yeah, well. We'll see if she sticks with it." Looking embarrassed, Evie began playing with her shoelace.

*　　*　　*

A few days later Molly was once again eating in the dining hall with Lucy, Evie, Casey Smithers, and Peter Jacobs. It was nice to be able to sit with all her friends and get caught up on the school gossip. Most of the kids were talking about parents' weekend, either with anticipation or with dread.

"The last time my mom was here, she flirted with Mr. Thacker," Casey groaned.

"No!" Molly leaned forward, fascinated. "What did he do?"

"I don't think he noticed," Casey admitted.

"Maybe he was scared to notice, 'cause Ms. Thacker would kick his butt," Lucy commented with a giggle.

"I like having my folks come," Peter said, taking a bite of vanilla pudding. "I show them my room, and all over school. They like it, too. I bet they would come more often if they could."

Molly listened enviously. Even if he were alive, her father probably wouldn't have been able to leave his film location just to fly to Boston for parents' weekend. But she would be so ecstatic if she could even pretend that it was a possibility. At times like this she felt so incredibly alone and different. She had felt a little weird before, when she had a father but no mother. Now she was completely apart from everyone else. Feeling a dull, familiar ache of sadness, she slowly crumbled her bread onto her tray.

33

*   *   *

Toby Daniels poked his head around the door
into the large workroom that Leslie Banks had set
up on one of the upper floors of the townhouse. It
was full of tall metal shelves stacked with film canisters, and there were three large editing machines.
Leslie was working on one now, her eyes squinting
in concentration, her hair tucked behind her ears.

"Excuse me, Les," Toby said.

"Yeah?" Leslie looked up impatiently.

"Phone call. It's Richard Price."

Leslie's eyes widened and she snapped off the editing machine light. Then she raced out of the
workroom and down the hall to her private study.
*Please let him have good news. Please let him tell me where
Molly is. Please, please . . .*

"Hello?" she said breathlessly into the phone.

"Hello, Ms. Banks? Richard Price."

"Yes, I know. Do you have any news for me?"
Richard Price was supposed to be one of the best
private investigators available, but so far it had just
been one disappointment after another.

"Well, it's not much, and it may turn out to be
nothing. But I've found a Molly *Stuart* in San
Francisco."

Leslie sat down at her desk, realizing that her
hand was trembling.

"The name is spelled differently, and I can't get
much information out of these people. It's probably

34

not the right girl, but I'm flying out there to see."

"Oh, good," Leslie breathed. "That's great, Mr. Price. We'll all keep our fingers crossed." If this *was* the right girl . . . Leslie hardly let herself admit the possibility. But it would be so wonderful. Every day that went by without word of Michael's daughter was sheer torture. Leslie *had* to find her—she had promised.

"I'll call you from San Francisco. Don't get your hopes up."

"Yes. Thank you, Mr. Price." Leslie hung up the phone and leaned back in her desk chair, feeling excitement race through her. What if it *was* the right girl? What if she had finally found Michael's missing daughter? *Oh, Michael, I'm trying. I'm really trying. I won't let you down.*

At the beginning of parents' weekend, classes were dismissed an hour early so that students could greet their visitors in the main hall. In all the commotion, Ms. Thacker had forgotten to assign extra work for Molly and Evie, so they had the luxury of a few free hours. Lucy begged them to wait with her for her parents.

"They've been so weird lately—I haven't even talked to them in two weeks," Lucy said. "I just don't want to be stuck with them alone. Maybe if you guys are here, too, they'll be on their best behavior."

Molly agreed, but inside she cringed every time a student was enfolded into a parent's warm embrace. She hungered for the feel of her own father's hug. Actually, she realized, she needed any kind of hug from anyone who truly cared about her. For just a second she allowed herself to wonder what a mother's hug felt like. Heaven, probably. Could anything feel better? she wondered. Wistfully she brushed her fingers across the small gold locket she always wore around her neck. It contained two tiny pictures of her mother and father when they were young. It was all she had.

An hour went by, and the main hall cleared out a lot as students took their parents on tours of the school.

Lucy looked at her watch and frowned. "I'm sure they know about parents' weekend," she said. "The school mentioned it in the last newsletter."

"They'll come," Molly reassured her. "They're probably just stuck in traffic or something."

Suddenly Evie gasped and clutched Molly's arm.

"Oh, no!" she whispered. "I don't believe it. Quick, where can I hide?"

Molly stared down at Evie, who was crouching next to her, trying to disappear behind a big chair. "What is the matter with you?"

"Hide, hide!" Evie repeated urgently. "Don't give me away."

Glancing around, Molly couldn't see what was

making Evie act so bizarrely. Then she noticed an attractive middle-aged woman, wearing a navy-blue business suit, looking around uncertainly. The woman reminded Molly of someone, but she couldn't think who. Suddenly she realized who the woman looked like. She looked like Evie.

"Evie!" Molly whispered. "Is that your mom?"

"Oh, no," Evie moaned again from behind the chair.

Molly looked at Evie's mother curiously. She'd heard all kinds of awful stories about her, but this woman didn't look so bad. In fact, she was pretty, and looked nice. She was wandering around the main hall, apparently searching for Evie. She seemed shy and unsure of herself, and was holding a copy of the school newsletter.

Making a quick decision, Molly yanked her arm free from Evie's nervous clasp. Leaving Evie writhing behind the chair, she walked across the room.

"Ms. Lucas?" Molly asked.

The woman looked startled, then gave Molly a tentative smile. From what Evie had said, Molly knew Ms. Lucas was only thirty-three years old, but she looked closer to forty. She had Evie's dark hair and dark eyes, but her face was tired and worn-looking. Her fingers clutched her purse nervously.

"Yes? Do I—do I know you?" she asked Molly in a husky voice.

"I'm Molly Stewart," Molly said, firmly shaking

Ms. Lucas's hand. "Evie's one of my best friends. She's been so excited about your coming."

Ms. Lucas smiled again, and Molly looked back to see Lucy dragging Evie out from behind the chair. Lucy began pushing Evie forward, a determined look on her face.

"Ah! Here's Evie now," Molly said brightly, ignoring her friend's angry scowl.

Ms. Lucas turned, and Evie quickly wiped the scowl off her face.

"Hi, Mom," Evie said unenthusiastically.

"Hi, sweetheart," her mother said. She made a move to hug Evie, but Evie pulled back a tiny bit. Then, as if realizing what she had done, she awkwardly gave her mother a quick hug.

Molly and Lucy stood there, feeling weird, but glad that Ms. Lucas had come.

"Well," Lucy said, giving Evie a meaningful look, "you'll probably want to take your mom on a tour. Show her the auditorium and gym and all."

Ms. Lucas smiled and nodded. "I'd like to see them. This place is . . . fancier than I thought it would be."

Molly grinned. "Parts of it are, anyway."

"Yeah, well, I might as well show you the classrooms," Evie said reluctantly.

She and her mother headed down the hall toward the outside doors. Molly could hear Ms. Lucas asking different questions about the school, normal parent-type questions. *Even Evie has a mother,* Molly realized with a start. Of course, she had always *known* that Evie had a mother, but it usually felt as though Evie's situation was just like Molly's. But it wasn't. Not really. Molly was in this alone.

"She seems nice," Lucy said, sounding almost surprised.

Molly nodded. "I just hope she doesn't let Evie down again."

"Speaking of being let down, have you noticed anything?" Lucy asked, taking off her glasses and cleaning them on the edge of her long shirt.

Molly looked around. "Like what?"

"Like the fact that it's almost dinnertime. Like the fact that my folks haven't shown yet."

With a little jolt of surprise, Molly realized it was true. All the other parents had come already. But where were the Axminsters?

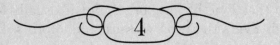

4

Romance and Riots

Later that night, after Ms. Lucas had gone home, the three girls met in Lucy's room. Lucy's roommate, Rachel Dawson, had gone out to dinner with her parents, who had come all the way from Minnesota to see her.

Lucy was trying to be nonchalant. "So I finally just called my parents," she said casually as Molly and Evie flopped on the twin beds.

"And?" Evie prompted.

"They *forgot*," Lucy said with exaggerated patience. "Actually, they didn't really forget—but my dad said that he assumed my mom was going, and my mom must have assumed that Dad would come."

"What did your mom say?" Molly asked.

"She wasn't there." Lucy rummaged under her bed and pulled out a bag of bite-size Snickers bars. Molly and Evie each took one. "She was out to dinner or something. Dad didn't really know. Anyway, he's moving into his own apartment next weekend."

"How weird," Molly commented. There was no use pretending it wasn't.

"Yep." Lucy looked embarrassed. "The whole thing is weird. I hate it. I hate thinking about it." She quickly unwrapped another miniature Snickers bar.

"What about you?" Molly nudged Evie with her foot. "Have you forgiven us for betraying you?"

Evie snorted. "No." She lay on her back and put her stockinged feet up against the wall, right on Lucy's Boyz II Men poster.

"It's just—well, she looked kind of uncomfortable, you know? I felt sorry for her," Molly explained.

Evie gently tapped her feet against the wall, humming a bit of Boyz II Men's latest hit. "Nah, it's okay," she said finally. "It was all right. I didn't show her my room or anything—didn't want to depress her. But she was . . . you know, okay."

"Good."

Lucy got up and put on a CD. Molly knew her friend was still upset about her parents. *I wonder how I would feel if Dad were alive, but an alcoholic, like Ms. Lucas,* Molly thought. She thought of all the pain Evie had been through because of her mother—the foster homes, the embarrassment. And now Lucy's parents were letting her down, too. They were in the middle of an icky divorce, and seemed to have forgotten all about Lucy. How would Molly feel if that were her father? Would she still miss him so much? Still love him so much? Still give anything to have him back?

Her fingers delicately traced the initials on her gold locket. Molly wasn't sure. But her heart said she probably would.

Two days later Molly was at the office supply store, getting some of the small pink Post-its that Ms. Thacker liked, when she ran into Toby Daniels. She hadn't seen him since he had brought her home almost two weeks before, though once she had seen his boss, the middle-aged woman. She thought his boss looked nice, just the right kind of owner for Mr. Tibbs.

She almost wanted to scurry out of the store before he saw her, but decided it would be rude, after he had been so nice to her that day. So after she had paid for her Post-its she walked over to where he was still waiting in line.

"Hi," Molly said shyly.

He looked down at her and smiled. "Hi, Anne! How have you been? I haven't seen you around lately."

It almost sounded as if he watched for her, Molly thought. She blushed a little when he used her fake name. Maybe she shouldn't have lied to him.

"I haven't had any errands lately," she replied.

Toby paid for his stuff and they walked out of the store together. "How come you're always the one running errands?" he asked.

"Work study," Molly said with a shrug. "How's M—uh, how's your cat?"

Toby laughed. "He's a goofball. The other day we found him playing with one of Leslie's diamond earrings. We were afraid he'd swallowed the other one. Thought we'd have to take him to be X-rayed."

"Oh, no," Molly said, grinning.

"But he was okay. It had just fallen onto the rug. He gets into everything, though."

"Yeah." Molly smiled, thinking about him. "Well, I have to go," she said, turning toward the dry cleaners.

"Okay. Take care, Anne." Toby gave her a friendly wave.

When Toby got back to the townhouse, he found his boss in a meeting with Richard Price.

"It was the wrong girl," Leslie Banks told Toby dully. "The one in San Francisco. She was a teenager. It wasn't Michael's daughter."

"Oh, I'm really sorry," Toby said sincerely. "But at least you're making some kind of progress, right? You're eliminating the prospects."

"Exactly," agreed Richard Price. "And we put an ad in the newspapers in New York, Los Angeles, London, and Paris."

"I bet someone will see the ad and call you,"

Toby said. "I know you'll find her, Les. Don't give up."

Leslie gave him a wan smile. "But what is she doing? How is she living? I lie awake nights thinking of how she feels, with her father dead . . ." Her voice shook. "Who's taking care of her?" Suddenly she slammed her fist down on the arm of her chair. "*I* should be taking care of her! I promised Michael on his deathbed! I'm failing him. . . ." She put her face into her hands and was silent. Over her head, Toby met Mr. Price's eyes. They looked worried.

"Spring Fling!" Lucy cried excitedly a few days later. She held up the latest copy of the *Glenmore Gazette* and waved it around.

"Say what?" Molly asked tiredly, taking a bite of scrambled eggs. A few days before, Evie's patrons had talked to Ms. Thacker about Evie's work study program. The result had been that Evie's hours had been cut back to six a week—practically nothing. Which meant that Molly had to handle even more. She'd gotten up at five o'clock this morning.

"Spring Fling," Lucy repeated. "It's the biggest dance of the year. It's usually the first weekend in April—so that's only six days away."

"This school seems to have dances at the drop of a hat," Molly said unenthusiastically. She poured herself more orange juice.

44

"Yeah. Too bad we haven't made it to any so far," Evie said with a mirthless laugh.

"Well, Molly went to the Halloween party, at least, before you came. But you both *have* to go to this one," Lucy said firmly. "It's the most important one. Everyone will be dressed up." She continued reading the article while she munched on her toast. "Hmm . . . it says here they still need people for the decorations committee and the music committee. Guess I'll do decorations. Evie?"

"Huh?" Evie looked up suspiciously.

"You have time to do something for the dance, since you're not working so hard. Sign up for the music committee, okay?"

"No." Evie frowned. "I hate stuff like that. I probably won't even go to this stupid thing. Anyway, I might not have time. Molly, I've been thinking. I actually kind of miss doing the newspapers and the breakfast stuff with you. Why don't I just keep doing it?"

Molly frowned at her. "Don't be stupid. You deserve to sleep late for once."

"Oh, and you don't?" Evie bristled.

Smiling, Molly reached out and punched Evie's shoulder lightly. "Look, thanks anyway. But enjoy your time off. It's no biggie." *It doesn't matter. You have a mother, a grandmother, and patrons. I don't have anyone. Of course I should do more stuff than you do.*

The end-of-breakfast bell rang, and the girls

45

brought their trays to the conveyor belt.

"So listen," Lucy said impatiently when they were out in the hall. "You guys aren't taking this seriously. We need to talk about what to wear."

"I don't *have* anything. Remember the class-portrait disaster?" Molly said.

"Hmm." Lucy frowned. "Okay, let me think about it."

"Hello, girls," Ms. Thacker said, passing them in the hall. "Are you excited about Spring Fling?"

"Yes," Lucy answered, looking at Ms. Thacker warily.

"Well, just remember it's a very formal occasion. The dress code will be strictly enforced." With a wintry smile the headmistress continued down the hall.

The three friends watched her for a few moments.

"Do you think she sleeps hanging upside down?" Molly asked, and Lucy and Evie cracked up.

"What now?" Leslie Banks fretted as an assistant knocked on her study door. Toby looked up from where he was showing his boss a section of film he had edited.

"Leslie?" A college-age girl poked her head in. "It's the man from Paramount."

"Oh, okay, Terri." Leslie waved her hand. "Show him in. I wanted him to see this rough cut of the film," she explained to Toby. "I think we're almost done—and it's the best thing Michael Stewart ever did in his life. If we can get a good distribution deal, it'll be the hottest thing since Rollerblades. And then I'll definitely have something concrete to give to his daughter. I want her to have everything that she deserves. Everything that he wanted her to have."

It was almost five-thirty on Saturday afternoon when Molly raced into Joe Brown's ice cream parlor. Just a few minutes before she had found a note shoved under the door of her room.

M.- Meet us right now at Joe Brown's! E. and L.

She found Lucy and Evie sitting in a back booth, empty ice cream dishes in front of them.

"What's up?" Molly asked breathlessly. She unzipped her jacket and pulled off her hat. It seemed to be almost spring now: in Fitzgerald Square tiny, pale green leaves were unfurling and getting bigger every day. There was no trace of snow on the ground, and crocuses and daffodils had been sprouting in window boxes and small sidewalk gardens.

"Ready for the dance tonight?" Lucy asked coyly.

Molly looked at her. "You know I'm not going," she said shortly. "I don't have anything to wear.

47

Remember the Spring Fling rule? Boys in ties and jackets, girls in skirts or dresses."

"I'm going," Evie said. She looked a little embarrassed. "My mom bought me a dress. It's not too bad."

"Well, I hope you guys have a great time," Molly said. She hadn't really minded the idea of not going to the dance, as long as she knew Evie wasn't going either. They had planned to stay upstairs and have their own private party, like they'd had on New Year's Eve. Now that Evie was going, Molly felt alone and left out. And Evie must have known for the past couple of days that she would be going, although she hadn't said anything. But Molly didn't want her friends not to go just because of her. "I bet it'll be really fun for you," she added, trying to put some enthusiasm in her voice.

Lucy and Evie just looked at each other and giggled.

"What?" Molly asked. All of a sudden she felt so strange—as if they were a club of two and she was an uninvited guest. But that was silly, she instantly scolded herself. They were her best friends.

"*Voilà,*" Lucy cried, taking a large shopping bag out from under the table. "Last night I figured out what to do. I can't lend you anything—you're taller and thinner than I am. And Evie doesn't have anything to lend either. So then I got this idea. I have a credit card. My parents don't really care what I buy with it, as long as it isn't a car or something.

Nowadays they probably wouldn't notice anyway."

"Lucy!" Molly was mortified. "You didn't buy me clothes, did you? There's no way I—"

Evie started giggling. "I told you she'd say that," she said to Lucy.

"Okay, okay," Lucy soothed. "Keep your shirt on. No, I didn't buy you clothes. I bought *me* clothes."

"I am completely lost here," Molly said.

"I just happened to make a mistake and bought the wrong size," Lucy continued. She glanced down at her watch. "Oh, gosh, look at the time. We have to get back for dinner. And after dinner," she told Molly, "we'll have to see if the dress I bought for myself just happens to fit you. By sheer coincidence."

"Oh, of course," Molly said dryly. "Coincidence." Part of her was embarrassed about Lucy feeling that she had to get Molly something to wear. After eleven years of having more clothes than she knew what to do with, it was strange to look pretty raggedy most of the time. But another part of her was really touched by Lucy's generosity and thoughtfulness. Lucy knew Molly needed something to wear, and she'd tried to give it to her in a way that wouldn't make Molly feel totally awful. She was a real friend.

"Ooh, girl!" Lucy eyed Molly critically as she pirouetted in front of Lucy's full-length mirror. "I have good taste, if I do say so myself."

"It's really great," Evie agreed.

The three girls were getting ready in Lucy's room before the dance. Lucy was wearing a maroon party dress with a lace collar. Evie was wearing a pretty flowered dress with cap sleeves and simple lines. It suited her, making her look prettier and more feminine than she usually did.

The dress Lucy had bought for "herself" was a white crushed-velvet tank dress. The slim lines suited Molly's tall, thin figure. She was wearing opaque white stockings and white flats—all mysteriously exactly her size.

"You look like a model," Evie said.

Molly just gazed in the mirror. It had been almost four months since she had worn anything really nice, and she'd almost forgotten what she used to look like. She looked different now—older, thinner, less cheerful.

"The dress is great," she told Lucy sincerely. "It's fabulous."

"Please say you'll wear it," Lucy pleaded. "We don't want to go without you."

"Okay," Molly said slowly, turning again in front of the mirror. "Twist my arm." She didn't want to let down Lucy and Evie. Just for one night, she would allow herself to pretend that everything was the way it used to be.

The gym was decorated with huge paper flowers, colored balloons, and upside-down umbrellas hang-

50

ing from the ceiling. A long banner was draped along one wall. SPRING FLING was painted on it in large green letters.

As soon as they walked in, Casey Smithers and Peter Jacobs came up to them.

"Hey!" Peter said, smiling widely. "It's about time you guys got here. Want me to show you the refreshment table? I was on the food committee."

"Sure," Molly said, smiling back. This was her very first school dance, and it seemed great so far. Loud music was playing from a sound system at one end of the gym, and lots of kids were already dancing. Everyone was dressed up, and the mood was festive.

After they'd all had a glass of punch, a boy from Lucy's math class asked her to dance. She headed out to the dance floor with him, grinning happily.

Then Peter asked Molly, and Casey asked Evie. Soon they were all dancing to a fast song in the middle of the gym.

"You look great!" Peter yelled over the loud music.

"Thanks!" Molly yelled back. She felt great, too. Just for that night, she was going to forget the sad turns her life had taken and pretend she was a normal kid going to a normal school dance.

After that song they switched partners, and Molly danced with Casey. He was making up all sorts of weird steps, and Molly tried to keep up with him. She couldn't even remember the last time she'd had so much fun.

Later they went back for more little sandwiches, cookies, and punch.

"Call me Cinderella," Molly told Evie, her face flushed with happiness and excitement. "This morning I was polishing silver in the kitchen, and now look at me." She laughed and took another bite of cookie.

"You look like Cinderella, too," Lucy said, giving Molly a big smile.

"Thanks to you," Molly said cheerfully. She no longer minded that she was in a borrowed dress and borrowed shoes. All that mattered was that she was having a good time with her friends.

The music was starting up again, and Molly headed back out on the floor with Jason Matthews, from her English class. Out of the corner of her eye she saw Celeste Foucher, dressed to kill and looking at least fifteen years old, greeting the Thackers, who had just come in. Ms. Thacker was smiling and saying hello to everyone, and complimenting students on their outfits.

But Molly refused to think about the headmistress. She knew she had completed every bit of work required of her, and now was her free time, her play time. She didn't have it very often, and she was going to enjoy it.

At the end of the song she smiled good-bye at Jason and went to find Evie and Lucy. They joined her coming off the dance floor, and for a few moments they stood on the sidelines, fanning themselves with Spring Fling napkins.

Peter came up, looking flushed and hot. He loosened his tie and threw his jacket over the back of a chair.

"Do you want to dance again?" he asked Molly.

"Sure," Molly said with a smile. She turned to put the napkin on a table and found herself face-to-face with Ms. Thacker.

"Molly. How nice you look."

"Thanks," Molly said uncertainly, and began to head off with Peter.

"One moment, Peter," the headmistress said, holding up her hand. "Molly, may I ask where you got your outfit?"

Surprised into silence, Molly only stared at Ms. Thacker.

Then Evie took a step closer, her face looking like a thundercloud. "Macy's," Evie said tightly.

"With what money?"

"Why do you want to know?" Evie said belligerently. Peter stood to one side, looking confused.

"Because, Eve," Ms. Thacker said deliberately, "if this dress was a gift to you from your patrons, I'm sure they'd be most distressed at the idea of your lending it to someone. And I know Molly didn't have the money to buy it. Are you saying it's stolen?"

Molly blushed with anger and embarrassment. "No!" she said, uncomfortably aware that a little crowd of students had gathered around and were whispering.

"It's mine, Ms. Thacker," Lucy said, stepping closer. "And I'm sure my parents would think it's okay." She crossed her arms over her chest.

"I disagree, Lucy," Ms. Thacker said, her brown eyes looking cold. "I believe I know your parents' wishes better than you do. And I think they wouldn't want you sharing your clothes with charity students."

Molly was only vaguely aware of an excited buzz going through the crowd of students. She felt mortified beyond belief. Was there any humiliation Ms. Thacker wasn't willing to put her through?

"Why don't you just leave her alone?" Evie cried, her fists clenched at her sides.

"Be quiet!" Ms. Thacker snapped. "Molly, you're dismissed. Please go to your room and put on your own clothes."

"But I don't have a skirt, or a dress," Molly protested, feeling as though she had plunged from the middle of a fairy tale to the middle of a nightmare.

"Then I'm sorry. But there will be other school dances."

"This is the last dance of the year," Peter objected, looking angry.

"That's enough, Mr. Jacobs. This doesn't concern you."

"It does! It concerns everybody!" Lucy looked as if she was about to burst into tears, she was so mad.

"Unfair!" Peter yelled, turning to the other students. "This is totally unfair!"

"I said that's enough!" Ms. Thacker was pale and rigid, her mouth fixed in a thin, angry line.

"It *is* unfair," someone in the crowd said timidly.

"There's no rule that says you have to wear your own clothes," someone else put in.

"*I'm* wearing *my* roommate's dress," a girl pointed out. "Who cares?"

Ms. Thacker faced the crowd of students, looking as if she were about to explode.

"Everyone stay out of this," she demanded harshly. "Go back to the party. This doesn't concern you."

"This is stupid," Casey Smithers said, coming to stand beside Peter. "You're just being mean to Molly."

"Shut up!" Ms. Thacker yelled. "Stay out of it!"

"It's okay, guys," Molly said urgently, trying to speak around Ms. Thacker. "I'll just go. It doesn't matter. No one else should get in trouble. Okay?"

"No!" someone cried from the crowd.

The next thing Molly knew, a cookie came sailing through the air and landed at Ms. Thacker's feet. The headmistress looked stunned. Then a paper cup full of punch hit the table beside her.

"Stop it!" Molly shouted. "All of you, stop it! Don't ruin the dance!"

But the crowd had already gone too far. Mr. Thacker rushed to his wife's side, holding up his hands in a placating gesture.

"Unfair!" someone yelled. "Unfair! Unfair!" other voices joined in.

"Okay," Mr. Thacker yelled, his mild voice sounding uncharacteristically stern. "Everyone just calm down. Let's get to the bottom of this. What's going on?"

"Unfair! Unfair!"

Molly felt tears welling up in her eyes as she looked helplessly out at the crowd of angry students. This was all her fault, for pretending to be something she wasn't. It had been a mistake, and now the whole beautiful dance was ruined.

"What's going on?" Mr. Thacker asked again. He looked over at Molly, as if she had the answer.

"I'm going," Molly choked out, her throat tight with the sobs she was holding back. "I'm going." Turning, she ran out the doors and across the playing field. The chilly night air brushed her hot cheeks and made her hair fly out like a golden curtain behind her. She could hear Lucy and Evie yelling her name, but she didn't slow down.

Minutes later she was pounding up the stairs to the fifth-floor attic. In her room she slammed the door, and braced her desk chair under the doorknob.

She didn't want to see anyone—not Ms. Thacker, not even Evie. Then she pulled off Lucy's beautiful dress and threw it on her desk.

Still sobbing, she pulled on her old flannel night-gown and climbed into bed in the dark. A shaft of moonlight came through the skylight and fell across the bed. Molly buried her face in her thin pillow and sobbed as though it were the end of the world.

She was crying so hard that she couldn't even hear the faint scratching sound at her skylight, or see the small, cat-shaped shadow outlined there. She couldn't hear the muffled curses of Toby Daniels as he cautiously crept across the roof after Mr. Tibbs, who had escaped from the townhouse attic once again.

Leslie Banks waited next to the townhouse's sky-light, whispering for Toby to be careful and for Mr. Tibbs to come back.

"This is what I get for working late," Toby mut-tered in disgust. "I get to chase stupid cats all across the roofs of Boston. Come here, Mr. Tibbs. Come here, boy."

Crawling on his hands and knees, and resolving to ask for a raise in the morning, Toby followed the fuzzy gray cat across Glenmore's roof.

"Come here, boy."

Mr. Tibbs was sitting by a skylight, and Toby re-alized that it was the same skylight he had first seen the little girl at. Now he realized something else: someone was crying in the attic, crying as though her heart were breaking.

Feeling guilty, Toby first got a good grip on Mr. Tibbs, then carefully leaned over to look in the window.

"Toby! What are you doing?" Leslie called anxiously. "Be careful."

It was a typical attic storage room, he saw, with junky furniture that no one could use. Then, as his eyes got used to the moonlight, he saw to his astonishment the neat stack of schoolbooks on the rickety desk. A pair of jeans was hanging on the closet doorknob. And there was a bed—a bed with someone in it.

Toby leaned farther over the window, and Mr. Tibbs squirmed to escape. The young man saw a slight form, the form of a child, huddled miserably in the bed. The thin shoulders were shaking, small hands were covering the face. Toby could distinctly hear the sound of wretched sobs.

Then the child moved restlessly in bed, angrily wiping at her face. A long ripple of golden hair fell over the side of the bed, and was highlighted by the moonlight. Toby gasped. It was Anne, the little girl who had run away! She really did live in the attic. Wait till he told Leslie.

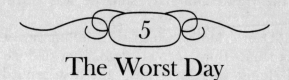

5

The Worst Day

The smell of lemon oil and furniture wax filled Molly's nose as she polished the carved wooden banister in the foyer of the main building. Occasionally students would walk by, looking at her curiously. Molly's face flushed, but she tried to ignore them.

Bing-bong. The doorbell rang, and Susan, Ms. Thacker's assistant, went to answer it. Glancing up, Molly saw a tall figure outlined in the doorway. The sun was behind him, making him hard to see, but he seemed so familiar. . . .

The person took two steps inside, and Susan closed the door behind him. Molly stared at him, feeling all the blood rush out of her face. It couldn't be. It couldn't be.

The man stepped forward, his brown eyes peering at Molly. He was older-looking, gaunt, as if he had been ill. The sun-streaked blond hair she remembered so well was longer and needed brushing.

The polishing rag dropped from her hand, and

Molly floated downstairs. Her eyes were devouring the figure hungrily, and he was staring at her, too.

"D-Dad?" Molly whispered, feeling as if she might faint. "But . . . you're dead. They told me so."

"I almost thought I was," the man replied, his voice harsh and rougher than she remembered. "But here I am. I've come to take you home."

In the next moment Molly was enfolded in his strong, wiry arms, her face buried in her father's shoulder as they hugged each other tightly.

"What's going on here?" Ms. Thacker's cool tones snapped Molly's head back. The headmistress saw Molly's father, and her eyes widened. "Mr. Stewart?"

"My father's come back," Molly said triumphantly. "He's come to take me away. And I'm going to tell him everything you did to me, everything you said."

The headmistress paled, and her slim hand went to her throat.

"Everything," Molly said firmly. "How you made me get rid of Mr. Tibbs. How you took all my stuff and sold it. How you gave Montana to Celeste Foucher. How you put me in solitary confinement. And how you humiliated me in front of everybody. You're evil and bad and I hate you! I hate you!"

The headmistress looked small and frightened as she drew back toward her office. The phone started ringing, and she turned to answer it. But after she picked it up, it kept ringing and ringing and ringing. . . .

Slowly Molly rolled over. Her hand went out automatically to claw her alarm clock into silence. A happy smile spread across her face as she remembered that her father was alive after all. She snuggled down into her blanket. She must be in a hotel, and he was right in the next room. . . .

Then a bedspring poked her in the back, and she realized her nose and hands were cold. Her eyes opened.

It was dark. It was chilly. The skylight whistled with the wind swirling in through the cracks in its frame. She was in her attic room, it was five o'clock in the morning, and it was time for her to get up and head downstairs to do the Sunday newspapers.

Her father was still dead. Spring Fling had been the night before. A wave of despair swept over Molly, so intense that it physically hurt. Her chest ached, her stomach muscles were sore from crying so hard the night before, her throat felt closed, and her eyes were swollen and gritty.

Slowly Molly climbed out of bed, shoving her feet into her old slippers. She padded across the hall to the bathroom and peered into the mirror by the light of its dim bulb.

Yep. She actually did look as bad as she felt.

And she felt as if she was at the end of her rope—the absolute end.

"You're sure it was Anne—the same little girl?" Leslie asked Toby. They both felt tired and grumpy after staying up so late the night before, working on the film. It had been almost two o'clock before Toby had made it to his own small apartment on the other side of town.

Now they were sipping hot coffee in Leslie's study, and talking about the little blond girl. Toby nodded in response to her question.

"Do you think she's truly being abused?" Leslie frowned.

"I don't know," Toby said with a shrug. "I don't think they're beating her. But why is she in that horrible attic, living like a . . . a rat or something? Where are her parents? And she's always running errands and stuff. And that day I found her in the train station—she just looked so lost. So hopeless."

"Poor thing," Leslie said quietly. Toby's description of the little girl's living conditions had practically broken her heart. She spent every minute worrying about Michael's lost daughter, not knowing how she was living or if she was all right. And here was this other little girl, right next door, who also didn't seem to have anyone who cared about her, anyone to take care of her. It was haunting Leslie. She'd been up half the night wondering what could be done—and she had to do something. Although her search for Michael Stewart's missing daughter had been fruitless so far, here was another little girl who needed help. And Leslie could at least help *her*—somehow. "What can we do, Toby? How can we help?"

"Ah!" Toby's face brightened. "I was thinking about it on the train home last night. And I have an idea."

That morning Susan, Ms. Thacker's assistant, sent Molly on a bunch of errands. Ms. Thacker hadn't asked to see Molly, hadn't spoken to her about what had happened the night before at the dance. Molly figured it was taking her some time to think up a punishment that was awful enough.

She sighed as she headed upstairs to put on an extra pair of socks before she went out. It was cold again. Spring was trying to come, but it was scared.

What are they going to do to me now? More solitary confinement? More work? Scream at me? Threaten me with—what? What do I have that they could take away? Molly felt tired and hopeless. She couldn't even imagine what would happen to her when she finally saw Ms. Thacker. All she could do was try to get through the day one minute at a time. Right now she had errands to run. Office supplies, some things from Woolworth's, a few kitchen things that Glenmore's cook, Mrs. Fulver, needed from a specialty market that was open on Sunday. This was Molly's life, the only life she had.

Outside, the weather was gray, harsh, and windy. On the corner of Fitzgerald Square, Molly paused to reread her list. The market was closer, but the groceries would be heavier to carry. She'd better get them on her way back. A sudden stinging sensation on her face caused her to look up in alarm. Freezing rain, not snow, pelted down from the sky and bounced off the cars and sidewalk.

Perfect, Molly thought glumly. *All I need now is to get run over by a truck, and my day will be complete.* Turning the corner, she waited at the stoplight to cross over to the main avenue. Molly bounced a little to keep warm.

"Here, little girl." A man suddenly paused and pushed a dollar bill into her hand. "Do you need help finding a shelter?"

Molly stared at him, astonished. With horror she realized he meant a shelter for homeless people.

"Oh! No—no, I'm fine," she stammered, trying to give him back his dollar. But he smiled and brushed her hand away, then headed in the other direction.

Stricken, Molly looked down at herself, at her worn, ill-fitting clothes and sneakers that were falling apart. She knew she sometimes looked a little shabby, but it was a shock to realize that she actually

64

appeared homeless. Shaking her head, she crossed the avenue and went to the office supply store.

After she had gotten the office stuff, she headed to Woolworth's, several blocks away. It was now lunchtime, and Molly was hungry, but she knew she didn't dare go back until she'd done everything on the list. She'd have to miss lunch.

The specialty grocery store was closer to home, but in the other direction. Molly sighed as she felt her feet, now wet and numb, growing heavier with each step. Her face was raw from the stinging sleet, and her bags seemed to be getting bulkier and harder to carry all the time.

At the next corner, Molly was about to cross when a taxi zoomed up next to the curb, spewing dirty water and ice across Molly's legs. With a gasp she looked down to see her jeans dripping with muddy slush. A man jumped out of the taxi and dug in his pockets for money, which he threw in to the driver. Molly's legs were now soaked and freezing, like the rest of her, and she felt close to tears.

This has got to be the worst day of my life, she thought wretchedly. But then she realized that it could be only the second worst. The worst was the day she'd found out about her father's death.

As the man slammed the taxi door and started to walk away, Molly noticed he'd dropped some money on the sidewalk.

"Hey, mister," she called, picking up the two dollar

bills and waving them at him. "You dropped this!"

The man turned around impatiently and yelled, "Keep it! I'm in a hurry!" Then he dashed off into an apartment building.

Well, why don't I just stand here and beg for a while? Molly thought in amazement. So far that day strangers had given her three dollars out of the blue. *I must look more pathetic than I thought.*

Then a happy realization crossed her mind. She had enough money for lunch, so it didn't matter if she missed the school meal. Her stomach rumbling in anticipation, she ducked into the first deli she came across. It was warm inside, though dirty slush was tracked across the floor from the ice storm. After carefully studying the prices, Molly got a Styrofoam cup of hot tea, another Styrofoam cup of hot vegetable-beef soup, and a toasted bagel. Feeling incredibly happy, she took her paper bag and headed out into the horrible weather.

Now I just need a dry place to eat, she thought. Maybe a trolley stop would do, if it had a little windbreak around it. There was one on the next block. Cheerfully Molly headed in that direction.

A dark, huddled form caught Molly's eye as she walked down the street carefully, trying not to spill her tea or soup. Molly stopped in her tracks. It was a homeless person, a *really* homeless person, curled up on the sidewalk next to a building. Icy sleet swirled around the blanketed figure. Bare, dirty toes peeped out from under the blanket. The person raised her head, and Molly saw it was a young woman. Even worse, she was holding a baby tightly in her arms, and trying to wrap the blanket more closely around it.

Molly stared at her, feeling the warmth of the hot food through its paper bag. *I'm not homeless,* she thought, watching the woman. *I might miss lunch, but I can have dinner later. I can even have seconds.* Molly's stomach rumbled, and the faint smell of soup curled up toward her nose. It smelled delicious.

Walking carefully toward the woman, Molly took the hot soup from the bag. Then she held it out, trying to smile. The woman looked at her dully, not comprehending.

"Take it," Molly said. "It's nice and hot."

Slowly a thin hand uncurled from beneath the blanket, and the woman took the cup and smelled it. She smiled, showing a few missing teeth. She nodded her thanks as she pulled off the lid. Then she propped the baby up and gently gave it a sip of soup.

"Careful," Molly said. "It's hot." She pulled her cup of tea out and put it on the ground next to the woman. "Hot tea." She hesitated for a moment, trying to ignore her rumbling stomach, then she handed the paper bag containing the bagel to the homeless woman.

"A bagel." Then, with a final little smile, Molly turned and headed down the block.

"Thanks, little girl," a voice called behind her. "Thank you."

Molly turned and waved, then kept on going across the street.

She's really desperate, Molly thought, hitching up her bulky packages. *I'm not really desperate.* But her stomach kept rumbling, and her packages seemed heavier than ever.

It was almost three o'clock when Molly finally returned to Glenmore. She had gotten everything on her list—maybe that would lessen Ms. Thacker's anger. After all, Molly *did* work hard. She always did as she was told, and tried to do a good job. Didn't that count for anything? In the foyer, the heat was on, and Molly stood in front of it, gently letting her frozen fingers absorb the warmth.

"There you are!" came Lucy's whisper. "I was worried about you—I was scared you'd tried to run away again."

Molly turned to her friend and smiled grimly. "I promised you and Evie I wouldn't. Anyway, I have nowhere to go." She picked up her bags and took them to the office, with Lucy tagging along beside her.

"Miss Stewart."

Here we go. Molly turned to see Ms. Thacker.

"Did you finish your errands?"

"Yes. I just need to give these groceries to Mrs. Fulver."

"Good. Please do so, then come see me in my

office." The headmistress turned and headed into her private room.

Lucy's eyes looked frightened as they took in Molly's pale, worn face. "Molly," she said softly. "What is she going to do? You can't go on like this."

"I have to," Molly said. "I have no choice. I can't stay on the streets by myself." Seeing Lucy's worried expression, Molly forced a smile. "Look, I'll see you at dinner, okay? I have to give Mrs. Fulver these groceries."

Lucy looked doubtful, but she nodded.

"Molly," Ms. Thacker said calmly, "Mr. Thacker and I have been discussing you at great length, as you may imagine."

Molly sat in the school office, facing the Thackers. It was almost dinnertime, and Molly was worn out from the hard day she'd had. She was very hungry.

"Frankly, I don't know what to do with you," Ms. Thacker continued. "I kept you here after your father's death out of the goodness of my heart. But you have proven remarkably ungrateful. You cross me at every turn, defy my wishes, and ignore your studies, and now it seems you are inciting others to defy me also."

Mr. Thacker shifted nervously in his chair, and out of the corner of her eye Molly saw him bite a fingernail. She didn't bother to defend herself

69

against Ms. Thacker's charges. What was the point?

"It is with great regret that I must tell you I've reconsidered my offer to keep you here as a charity student. Mr. Thacker and I have decided that you may remain here until the end of the school year. At that time we will relinquish our custody of you, and you will be put into foster care."

A great coldness seemed to pierce Molly's soul. Although she had feared this, somehow she hadn't ever really expected it to happen. Foster care. Evie had said such awful things about it. And she would probably never see Lucy or Evie again. Or Mr. Tibbs, right next door. All day, people had been mistaking her for a homeless person. Now she really would be. *Oh, Daddy—help me.*

"We're sorry, Molly," Mr. Thacker said awkwardly.

"Molly?" Ms. Thacker prompted. "Do you have anything to say?"

Molly searched inside, but truly couldn't come up with anything—no tears, no anger, very little feeling of any kind. This was it. This was the end of her world.

"Molly? Do you understand?" Mr. Thacker looked concerned.

"Yes," she said in a low voice. "I understand."

"Very well," the headmistress said. "I believe dinner is about to begin. You're dismissed."

*   *   *

"She can't!" Lucy gasped, leaning over the dining table.

"That witch!" Evie snarled. "I can't believe her!"

Molly made a face, though inside she was still shocked and numb. She felt sad as she looked at her friends' outraged faces, but that was all. "It wasn't only her. Mr. Thacker must have agreed. I didn't think I was such a horrible person, but . . ."

"You're not!" Lucy cried softly. "This is awful. What can we do?"

"Nothing." Weirdly enough, Molly felt calm and resigned to her fate. There was nothing left inside that would let her fight.

"I'm going to tell my parents," Lucy said firmly.

"I'm going to tell Melina and Philip Duke," Evie said.

"What could they do?" Molly asked. "They all have their hands full. And anyway, if they make the Thackers let me stay, can you imagine what my life would be like then? It's bad now, but if Ms. Thacker hated me twice as much . . ."

Lucy sat back, looking angry. "Well, this isn't over yet. There has to be something we can do. I'm going to think about it."

"Me too," Evie agreed. "We've got to come up with something. Hey, did you hear that Peter Jacobs didn't get punished? No one did, except you."

"And you're the one who was trying to get everyone to behave," Lucy added angrily.

Molly shrugged. "I'm glad he wasn't punished. I would have felt really bad about it."

"He wasn't the only one who stood up for you," Evie reminded her. "Anyway, they called his parents, but they didn't actually do anything to him. I guess they just want the whole Spring Fling incident to die down."

"The Spring Disaster, you mean," Lucy said dryly.

"The whole thing was my fault," Molly said unhappily.

Lucy immediately looked outraged. "It was not! If it was anyone's, it was Ms. Thacker's, for being such a total witch."

"Yeah. You had nothing to do with it, Mol," Evie insisted. "I can't believe they're going to make you pay for it like this. I just can't believe it."

"Me neither," Lucy said somberly.

"Believe it," Molly told her friends.

That night, as she was brushing her hair, getting ready for bed, Molly thought about her friends, and how lucky she was to have them. But even though they were her best friends in the world, they were still on one side of the fence, and she was on the other. In the end, they both had someone to stick up for them, to care about what happened to them, and she had no one. That was a huge difference, a difference that nothing could ever change—not loyalty, or love, or hope. Molly was entirely alone.

And there was nothing she could do about it. There was nothing she could do about anything. At the end of the school year, she would be sent into foster care.

As exhausted as Molly was, it still took her a while to fall asleep that night. The unseasonably cold wind was howling and rattling her skylight, as though it were determined to come in. The clouds passing over the moon made weird shadows on her walls and floor. Molly was cold, and she huddled up as best she could, tucking her hands under her arms and curling her feet together.

Finally, worn out by the cold and the long, hard day, she let her eyes close and her breathing relax.

Her last thought before she fell asleep was, *I told Lucy I would bear it, that I had to—but I know I really can't. I can't run away again, but I can't go on this way, either. I just won't make it.*

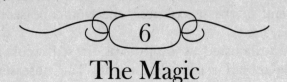

6

The Magic

That night Molly's mind betrayed her once again, letting her dream such a wonderful dream that it was sheer torture to wake up. For the first time in four months, she dreamed that she actually felt toasty and warm under her covers.

Oh, I don't want to wake up, she thought, stretching her feet out and feeling nothing but cozy warmth. *Please don't let me wake up for a while.* She knew any minute her hated alarm clock would go off, piercing the chilly air with its shrill buzz, but right now she just felt so comfortable . . .

Slowly, against her will, a noise penetrated her consciousness. It was a humming sound, like a small motor or fan. It clicked on, ran for a while, then clicked off. Molly frowned without opening her eyes. What could that be? She didn't have anything in her room that could make that sound.

The noise clicked on again, and Molly sighed, knowing she was truly awake and that nothing could make her go back to sleep until she stopped the noise. Reluctantly she opened her eyes, hating for the shock of coldness to end her dream of warmth.

Her room was dark, with only a wide stripe of moonlight slanting in through her skylight. Molly sniffed the air experimentally. She frowned. Her nose felt warm—not freezing and runny like it usually did. Leaning over a bit, she looked at her alarm clock. It was not quite five o'clock. What had woken her up? She pulled the covers up around her shoulders. Then she paused. What had happened to her blanket? It felt . . . soft. Thick. Cozy. But that was impossible. She and Evie each had one ancient, ragged blanket of rough, scratchy wool that barely kept them warm. This cover felt completely different.

Like a comforter.

Molly heard the small whirring sound again. That did it. She slid out of bed, couldn't find her slippers, and went across the room barefoot to snap on her desk lamp. Then she gasped.

She *was* still dreaming—she hadn't woken up yet, after all. The previous night she had gone to sleep in a room that was ugly, bare, and cold, and now . . .

The whirring noise was from a small, powerful space heater set on the floor. Molly found its instruction booklet on her desk. Also on her desk was a pretty, floral-pattern stationery set—a desk mat, pencil holder filled with pencils and pens, and a little address book and diary.

75

Her bed was hardly recognizable: the scratchy blanket had been replaced by a soft, warm comforter, and a new fluffy pillow lay at the foot of the bed. A thick, quilted bathrobe was draped across the rusty footboard, and Molly found warm, fuzzy slippers where her old ones had been. There was even a set of brand-new flannel pajamas neatly folded on her chair. Molly looked down at where her wrists were coming out of her old, thin nightgown, and she laughed softly.

Then she noticed the walls. Colorful posters of flowers, animals, and nature scenes had been tacked to the walls with fine, sharp pushpins. They covered the worst of the cracked, dirty plaster.

There was even a soft throw rug by her bed, with a delicate rose pattern on it, and another one in front of her closet.

Oh, it's just too wonderful, Molly thought. *I hope I never wake up. I hope I just sleep forever and keep living this wonderful, magical dream.*

For that was what it was, Molly had realized at once. It was magic. She had seen magic before, in her dad's movies—seen people's wishes come true, and miracles happen, and happy endings. The fact that they were all special effects made no difference. Once it was up on the screen and everyone was seeing it and believing it, that was all that mattered. That was what had happened here. Magic.

Suddenly Molly's knees felt weak, and she sank

down onto her bed. That was when she saw the wicker picnic hamper on the rug in the middle of the floor. She pushed her feet into her fuzzy new slippers, and tied the belt of her new robe around her waist. Then she opened the hamper. It had a large thermos in it. Molly unscrewed the top and sniffed. Hot chocolate! Real hot chocolate, not from a mix. There were also several muffins, and miniature jars of jam and butter. Inside the hamper, pinned to the blue gingham lining, was a small envelope.

Molly opened it with trembling fingers. The envelope contained only a plain white card, on which was typed a message.

For the little blond girl
From a friend

Oh, my gosh, Molly thought, sitting on her warm floor in front of the hamper. Instinctively she reached for the gold locket that she never took off. Her hand held it tightly, as though it could somehow keep her rooted to earth. *This is real—all of it. It's here. I can eat these muffins and drink this hot chocolate. It's real—as real as I am.* She felt stunned—she simply didn't know what to think. She had a friend. But how could this have happened? Molly couldn't even imagine who could have done all this. Lucy? No. Not even Lucy.

Molly leaped to her feet and opened her door

quietly. It was so early that none of the housekeeping staff was up yet. Carefully Molly crept down the dark, cold hall to Evie's room, and let herself in without a sound.

It took several shakes on Evie's shoulder to get her to wake up. Like Molly, she was cold, and had curled into a tight little ball to sleep. Reluctantly she uncurled and peered at Molly with one groggy, half-closed eye.

"Mol? Whatsa matter?" She huddled under her blanket, then opened her other eye. "You want me to help with the papers?"

Molly smiled. "No—don't be silly. But you have to come to my room. It's important."

Now Evie sat up a little, looking concerned. "You're running away again?"

"Of course not. Now come on." Laughing, Molly pulled back the covers. Evie instantly curled up again, trying to pull her thin nightgown around her to keep out the frigid air.

Molly grabbed her hand and tugged. "Come *on*." Silently the two girls sneaked back down the hall to Molly's room.

"What are you wearing?" Evie whispered, fingering the new bathrobe. "Where did you get this? Is it Lucy's?"

"You'll see." Molly wiggled her eyebrows at her friend, then let her door swing open quietly. They entered. For a brief, hysterical moment, Molly worried that she really had imagined everything, and that it would all be gone and Evie would think she was totally nuts. But it was still there—every bit of it. The food, the rugs, the blankets. And the room was warm and inviting.

After quickly pushing her towel against the crack beneath the door, Molly looked at Evie. Her mouth had dropped open, and she was standing there like a statue, her dark eyes looking around wildly, taking it all in.

"Molly!" she breathed, reaching out to touch the desk set. "Where did you get this stuff?" She looked almost horrified. "Mol, you didn't . . . I mean . . . of course you didn't *steal* this stuff, right?" Evie cast her a worried glance.

Molly punched her in the arm. "Eeevieee! Good grief. Of course not! At least, not unless I've been sleepwalking. That's the totally weird thing—when I went to sleep last night, none of this was here. Just now I woke up, and here it all is. What do you think it means?"

Evie's dark eyes bored into hers. "I think we'd better quit eating so much of Lucy's chocolate. It's rotting our brains and making us see things."

Grinning, Molly dragged Evie down on the rug in front of the heater and handed her the card. Evie automatically turned toward the heat as she read it, almost purring with contentment.

"Ooh, nice," she murmured.

"And look." Molly pulled out the thermos and the plate of muffins. "You can use my mug, and I'll use the thermos cap."

Two minutes later they were sipping the hot chocolate and eating muffins. In the middle of their meal, Molly's alarm went off, and she ran over to turn it off.

"I only have a few minutes before I have to get downstairs," she said. "Today's the first day I won't mind doing all my stupid chores."

Evie swallowed a bite of muffin. "But how did this happen? Where did it come from?"

"Beats me." Molly shrugged happily. "I can't even think how anyone could do it. Who could get all this stuff up the stairs without being seen?"

"I don't know. It's not like the *Enterprise* beamed it down."

Molly giggled. "But it's almost that weird. The card said it was from 'a friend,' but I don't have a clue who that is. And right now I don't care. It's all just too fabulous."

Standing up, Molly screwed the cap back on the thermos, then quickly got into her everyday clothes.

"I'd better get downstairs to do the papers and breakfast," she said. "But why don't you go back to sleep for an hour? Just get into my bed here and set the alarm. Then, when you wake up, you'll be all warm and toasty."

"Sounds tempting," Evie said, eyeing Molly's new comforter.

80

"Go on," Molly urged. "I'll see you downstairs at breakfast."

Evie bounced a little on the edge of Molly's bed. "Ouch," she said automatically as she hit the bedspring. "Okay, I will, Mol. Thanks so much for coming to get me. I think that hot chocolate will keep me going all day."

"You and me both," Molly said, grinning as she closed the door behind her.

Ms. Thacker had assumed that Molly would appear subdued and unhappy the day after she'd found out she was being put in foster care. There was a chance she might be humble—apologetic, even. Maybe she would ask the headmistress to rethink her decision. No doubt, Ms. Thacker thought, Molly would look red-eyed and miserable, lost and alone.

Which is why it was so completely disconcerting to find Molly humming cheerfully under her breath as she filled silverware trays from the dishwasher in the kitchen.

"Molly!" Ms. Thacker said.

Molly looked up, surprised. Ms. Thacker hardly ever came into the kitchen.

She looks almost happy, Ms. Thacker saw with amazement. *She looks rested and rosy-cheeked and clear-eyed.* With a rush of anger, Ms. Thacker wanted to reach out and wipe the healthy glow off her face.

"You *do* remember our talk yesterday?" the

headmistress said. "I haven't changed my mind, you know. At the beginning of June, you're leaving Glenmore for good."

She was rewarded by a troubled look coming into Molly's eyes. Sometimes Cathy Thacker wondered why she felt so hostile toward Molly, but she still didn't know. Ever since Molly had shown up at the beginning of the school year, so obviously rich, so obviously spoiled, so obviously used to moving in circles that Ms. Thacker only read about, she had rubbed the headmistress the wrong way. And certainly the girl had done nothing to redeem herself since then.

"I haven't forgotten," Molly said quietly. "I understand."

"Well, you look as if the idea doesn't bother you at all," Ms. Thacker continued.

Molly didn't respond. One of the kitchen assistants, Julio, came over and wordlessly set down another tray of silverware. Ms. Thacker ignored his slight frown. It was none of his business. If he didn't like her policies, he could take a hike.

"Is there anything you want to say?" Maybe, just maybe, if Molly started crying or begging for mercy . . . there was a very slim chance Ms. Thacker would relent. The girl was *somewhat* useful, after all.

But Molly did neither—only looked thoughtful and shook her head.

Feeling angrier than ever, Ms. Thacker turned on her heel and stalked out of the kitchen. The nerve of that girl! The sooner she was gone, the better. This whole school year had been disrupted because of Molly. First because she was so rich and her father made so many demands, and then because she was so poor and so completely uncontrollable. Well, six more weeks, and Cathy Thacker would never have to look into those superior green eyes again.

In the kitchen, Molly was aware that everyone had stopped working to look at her. If they hadn't heard before that she was being sent away, they knew it now. A slight flush rising in her cheeks, Molly went back to filling silverware trays. One by one the people around her went back to work, but Molly knew they were looking at each other in bewilderment.

It had been such a great morning until the headmistress showed up, Molly thought, suppressing a sigh. But even though Ms. Thacker had done all she could to ruin Molly's day, Molly still had the memory of waking up to find her room filled with presents and beautiful things. She remembered sitting on the rug with Evie, drinking hot chocolate and eating wonderful muffins. She would always have that memory. Nothing Ms. Thacker did could take it away. As she filled the teaspoon section of the tray, Molly couldn't help smiling again, just a little.

That day, despite Ms. Thacker, it was as if Molly had finally found her way into the sunshine after an endless season of gray skies and snow. Her classes seemed easier, people seemed friendlier—things simply weren't as difficult. When she and Evie passed each other in the halls, they winked and grinned. All day long, thoughts kept humming through Molly's brain: *I have a friend. Someone cares about me. Someone cares if I'm happy or not.* It was like wearing a warm, snuggly cloak.

As Molly and Evie shuffled through the lunch line Evie whispered, "Are you going to tell Lucy?"

Molly nodded. "Of course. It's just . . . I thought I'd tell her tomorrow. Because, you know, maybe it was just for one day. Just to get me over the hump. The stuff might not be there tonight. And I thought, if it isn't, I don't want to be all excited about it to her. I'll tell her tomorrow, whether it's still there or not."

"Uh-huh. I understand."

They grabbed their trays and headed for their usual table. A few moments later Lucy joined them, looking glum.

"Hey, guys." She plopped down in her seat and poured herself a glass of milk.

"What's wrong?" Evie asked.

"You mean, what's *right?*" Lucy said. "I'm still totally bummed about Molly getting kicked out, and on top of everything else, I have to meet with my parents' lawyers in a couple of days."

"What for?" Molly began cutting up her baked potato.

"To decide who I want to live with," Lucy said. "What am I supposed to say? Neither one of them could care less. Maybe I'll just join you at your foster family, Mol."

"Come on, Lucy," Molly said briskly. "It's not that bad. Maybe the lawyers will tell you that you'll have shared custody. You have to remember that you *do* actually have real parents. That's something special. Don't just throw them away. My foster family isn't going to be a joke, you know."

Lucy ate in silence for several minutes, looking thoughtful. Finally she sighed and put down her fork. "You're right," she told Molly. "You're totally right. I'm being stupid. I have it better than a lot of kids, even with everything that's going on. And of course your foster family isn't a joke. I'm sorry." She gave Molly a smile. "If you hear me being so stupid again, you have my permission to kick me."

"It's a deal," Evie said cheerfully.

"Okay, now, what do we have today?" Leslie Banks started rummaging through the large shopping bags that she and Toby had lugged into the workroom.

"Um, books, CDs, the CD player . . ." Toby pulled out a small stuffed bear. "A teddy bear." He grinned. "She's not too old for this, is she?"

Leslie looked up, blowing her hair out of her face. "How would I know? I don't know anything about kids." *All I know is that I would give anything to see one kid, soon. Oh, Molly Stewart, where are you? I need to see you, need to know you're okay. I want to tell you everything your dad said about you.*

"Earth to Leslie," Toby was saying patiently. "Let's take all the price tags off this stuff. We'd better hurry. It's dark already, and I'm not sure what time she'll be back."

He briskly wrote a quick note, leaning on one of the books.

"Wait—what did you say?" Leslie asked, reading the note over his shoulder.

To Anne
From your friend

"Oh, no, let's not use her name," Leslie said. "We didn't the first time, did we?"

Toby shook his head. "No. We just said 'for the little blond girl.'"

"Let's use that again," Leslie said decisively. "I feel like if we use her name, she'll know that her friend is someone who knows her in real life. But if we say 'to the little blond girl,' it seems more . . . I don't know. More magical."

Grinning, Toby nodded. "Okay, we won't use her name. Now I'd better get this stuff bundled up."

Molly didn't get upstairs until almost nine o'clock

86

that night. She hadn't seen Evie since dinnertime. In the dark hallway in front of her door, she paused. What if it had all been taken away? What if it really had been just for one night and one night only?

It wouldn't matter, Molly thought, biting her lip. She'd had it for one day, and that had been enough. Now she knew that someone, somewhere, had cared about her for one day. She took a deep breath, threw her shoulders back, and opened her door. Then she gasped.

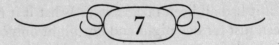

7

Springtime at Last

The magic was still there. In fact, it had done even more. There were colorful cushions tied on to her rickety desk chair, so it would be more comfortable. Now she had *two* fluffy pillows on her bed. A floor lamp with a floral-patterned shade cast a warm glow throughout the room. On the rug by her closet was a small TV table with a tablecloth on it, and more food. Two small folding chairs with pillows on them were waiting by the table. There were even several paperback books resting on a small table by her bed.

Molly couldn't react at first. Her first thought was, *Someone still cares about me.* Without warning, fat tears welled up in her eyes and spilled down her cheeks. An overwhelming feeling of gratitude threatened to burst right out of her skin. Deep inside, she worried that somehow she *was* dreaming all this, making it up, and it wouldn't last. But when she felt the heat from the small heater, smelled the food that had been left behind, and flipped through her new books, she felt more convinced.

In seconds she had yanked open her closet door and called through to Evie. When Evie ran down the hall and burst through the door, Molly simply waved around at everything, unable to speak for a moment.

"Who is it, Evie?" Molly asked softly, starting to open the food packages. "Who could be so good to me?" She looked up, her green eyes wide.

"It looks like they don't want you to know," Evie said, sitting in one of the folding chairs. "Just take it and be happy."

"I'm trying."

That night Molly and Evie shared more hot chocolate. The yucky old radiator had been turned off and topped with a board that was covered with a pretty tapestry-print cloth. On it they found an electric hot-water kettle and a selection of teas and hot drink mixes. There were also packets of cookies, dried fruit, granola bars, and other good snacks that wouldn't spoil.

When Molly went to bed, she found a new futon on her bedframe. For the first time in four months, she didn't have to worry about bedsprings poking her in the back. *Oh, thank you, thank you, whoever you are.*

"I saw her this afternoon," Leslie Banks said conspiratorially a few days later.

"Yeah?" Toby Daniels sat up, his blue eyes looking interested.

"Saw who?" Terri, Leslie's other assistant, looked up from her paperwork.

"Just a friend of ours," Leslie said with a smile. Later, when they were alone, she told Toby the whole story.

"I was at the dry cleaners, and she came in to pick up something. I can't believe someone is making that child pick up her dry cleaning," Leslie added indignantly.

"Well, they're making her live in an attic—why not pick up dry cleaning?" Toby said, a disgusted tone in his voice. "But how did she look?"

"Better," Leslie said triumphantly. "Definitely better. She seemed less washed out, less beaten down. I think your plan really made a difference."

"*Our* plan. It's been fun," said Toby. "You should come across the roof with me sometime, just to watch her expression when she opens her door to find something new. It's really great."

Leslie groaned. "There is no way you're getting me on that roof," she said firmly. "As much as I'm enjoying helping our little friend." She checked her watch. "Speaking of little girls, Mr. Price is due any minute. I just pray he has some news for me. I love helping Anne, but the thought of *my* little girl, who might not have anyone to help her, makes me feel desperate." Sighing, she brushed her fine hair back and headed to her office.

                    *   *   *

That day when Molly was out running errands
after school, she felt as if spring were wrapping its
arms around her. Her jacket was almost too warm,
and the air had a damp freshness very different from
winter's brisk chill. Taking a shortcut through
Fitzgerald Square, she saw that the trees were now
completely covered with leaves, some almost as big
as her hand. People were walking their dogs along
the snowless paths, and even the dogs themselves
seemed extra bouncy and excited about the weather.

Spring, Molly thought, walking along in her
beat-up, too-small sneakers. *A new start.* The magic
had begun in spring, and spring was when she'd
found out that soon she'd be living somewhere else,
with different people. She still felt scared about
going into foster care. But she couldn't feel depressed anymore, not when she had a mysterious
friend who cared about her. Maybe foster care would
be better than Glenmore. Maybe her new family
would be loving and good to her.

That night Lucy sneaked upstairs with Evie and
Molly.

"Jeez, it's still freezing up here," Lucy whispered
as they tiptoed down the hall to Molly's room.

"Just wait," Molly said with a grin as she opened
the door to her room.

Warm air rolled out into the hallway. Molly
turned the portable heater off during the day for

                           91

safety, but it gave so much warmth that her room was always toasty when she came in at night.

The three girls stepped inside. Molly could feel Lucy's surprise at what she saw.

"This is the magic," Molly explained. "What we were telling you about. It started a couple of days ago, and it seems like it's here to stay."

Lucy stared around her, her mouth open in astonishment. "But where did it come from?" she finally gasped. "Who did all this?"

Molly shrugged. "I don't know. We can't figure out how they did it at all. I don't want to know—it would spoil the magic somehow."

"Well, it's fabulous," Lucy declared happily, bouncing on Molly's new futon. "Wow, look at your CD player. And CDs! I can't believe it. It's so romantic, like something out of a book. How can we find out who it is?"

"Oh, please don't try," Molly begged. "It really would ruin everything. I feel like my fairy godperson—that's what I've been calling whoever it is—doesn't want to be found out. Promise me you won't try."

"Oh, okay," Lucy agreed, "but I'm dying of curiosity."

"Me too. But we'll just have to live with it," Molly said.

She fixed them each a cup of hot herb tea, and they sat on Molly's bed. The whole room was comfortable and cozy.

"What happened with the lawyers?" Molly asked Lucy. "We missed you at dinner."

"That's what I wanted to tell you," Lucy said. "It was really weird. Both my folks were there. But it was like my mom wasn't even pretending to be that interested. Get this—my dad said he wants full custody. He said Mom could have visiting rights if she wanted."

"Visiting rights! What did she say?" Molly exclaimed.

"It seemed okay with her," Lucy reported. "I mean, she didn't argue about it or anything."

"Usually the mother gets custody," Evie said, taking a sip of tea.

"Usually they aren't dealing with *my* mother," Lucy said dryly. "Actually, I wasn't that surprised. I mean, she's always been okay to me—she's not mean or anything. But I always sort of felt like one of her dogs. You know, she cares about me, but in a weird way. Like I was a pet, not a kid."

"What about your dad? Do you want to live with him?"

Lucy looked thoughtful. "Yeah, I think so. He says he wants to get a big apartment here in Boston. He even said that next year I could go to day school, if I want to, and live at home."

"Wow!" Evie looked impressed. "You think he means it?"

"I guess so. He doesn't usually say stuff he

doesn't mean. So we'll see." Lucy shrugged. "It's just so weird, knowing I won't have my same old room anymore. I'll have a new room in a new apartment."

"Yeah, but all your stuff will be there. And at least you won't have to shuttle back and forth between two different houses—a week here, a week there," Molly pointed out.

"That's true," Lucy said, nodding. "I know lots of kids who have to do that."

They sat in comfortable silence for a while, sipping their tea and eating cookies.

"My mom's looking for an apartment," Evie said finally.

"Really? Good for her," Molly said. She wanted to ask if Evie would go live there, but sometimes it was hard asking Evie personal things.

"Hey," Lucy said, her round face brightening. "Wouldn't it be wild if next year I lived with my dad, Evie lived with her mom, and Molly lived with her foster family, and we all went to the same day school?"

Evie snorted. "Earth to Lucy. Number one, I'm not going to go live with my mom, ever, no matter what she says. Number two, you'd probably be going to a fancy private school with uniforms or something, and Molly and I definitely wouldn't be."

Lucy looked deflated, and Molly patted her shoulder. "It was a nice thought, anyway," she told Lucy. "It would have been fun."

Soon it was time for Lucy to sneak back downstairs before lights out. Before she left she looked around Molly's transformed room one last time. "This is really amazing," she said. "Let me know what happens tomorrow."

"You got it," Molly said. After her friends left, Molly changed into her warm flannel pajamas, turned off her heater, and got into her comfy, warm, snuggly bed. *Spring,* she thought sleepily. *Spring is a time for new beginnings. For me, for Lucy, and for Evie. I hope we can stick together.*

The next day Ms. Thacker announced that Molly no longer had to work in the kitchen before meals, because new kitchen help had been hired. In a way, Molly was almost sorry, because she had been learning how to do all kinds of things in the kitchen. She'd even been thinking that when she got out of school she could maybe work in a restaurant. She had no idea what else she'd be able to do.

"But I guess I can get a job at a plant nursery," Molly muttered to herself that afternoon. Her replacement chore was to work in the Alumni Garden, which was a pretty, old-fashioned garden that faced Fitzgerald Square. On one side was the main building, and on the other side was the wall of the auditorium.

Old Ben, the gardener and general handyman, had asked her to weed some of the beds. Her leather gloves were too big, and her knees ground into the damp

95

earth, getting her pants so dirty that Molly would probably never get the marks out. But she didn't really mind it. She liked plants and growing things, and it was nice to be outside in the warm spring weather.

Over the next week she helped Ben rake the narrow paths, trim the hedges, and repaint the iron benches. It was hard work, and Molly got sweaty and dirty, but it seemed impossible for her to feel down. Every day she saw her good friends; she was actually keeping up, more or less, with all her classes; and she had the magic. How could she be unhappy?

In some ways, knowing Ms. Thacker was putting her into foster care had taken a lot of pressure off. Molly didn't have to worry about her grades as much; she didn't have to walk on eggshells. Even though she was worried about what awaited her in foster care, at least she didn't have to worry about what awaited her at Glenmore any longer.

During these weeks in April, Molly felt the icy shell that had surrounded her heart start to melt. Since her father had died, she'd been so desperately unhappy that she'd hardly allowed herself to feel anything. But now with the warmer weather, the sunshine, the outdoor work, and the magic, Molly could feel new life creeping through her veins like sap through a young tree.

Of course, she still felt miserable whenever she thought of her father. Molly missed him more than she could say, and thought about him all the time.

But she also felt that she just might make it after all. The magic was giving her hope. For the first time in so long she had something to look forward to at the end of each day—some new treat, a book, something good to eat. It gave her hope, made her feel special again. Molly truly felt that the magic, and her heavenly, mysterious friend, had saved her life.

One afternoon toward the end of April, Molly was weeding the front bed of the Alumni Garden. Right in front of her was the high wrought-iron fence that shut the garden off from the street. It was a pretty afternoon, and Molly was humming while she worked. People passed by on the other side of the fence, and Molly enjoyed watching them. Soon she would go inside, get washed up, and have dinner. Then she could look forward to going to her lovely room and studying at her desk, with its pretty desk set. Thinking about this, Molly broke into a little snatch of song.

"Hi, Anne!" said a voice on the other side of the fence.

Startled, Molly dropped her trowel, then smiled as she recognized Toby Daniels.

"I didn't see you at first, behind the hedge," he said. "I thought I was hearing things."

Molly grinned. "No, it was just me." She brushed a long strand of blond hair off her face, smudging her cheek with dirt. Again, she felt bad about giving him a fake name. She really should tell him her real name. He was nice.

"I haven't seen you for a while. How's everything?" Toby asked.

"Oh, fine," Molly said cheerfully. "I'm glad it's spring. How's . . . your cat?"

"Oh, he's great. Getting real big. Well, I'll see you later." With a little wave, Toby headed down the block toward the stone townhouse. He smiled to himself as he thought of Anne's face, now less pale, less pinched, less unhappy-looking than she had been before he and Leslie had put their plan into action. He liked having this secret, and he liked helping the little blond girl. She was a nice kid.

Then he frowned. Her face was happier, but the rest of her still looked like a ragamuffin. Her jeans were too short, and so was her sweater. Her shirt collar was worn and frayed, and her toes poked out of holes in her sneakers. Hmm. Maybe Leslie should do something about that.

8

Molly's Patron

One night at the end of April Molly and Evie took the elevator together to the fourth floor, then slowly climbed the steps to their fifth-floor attic.

"Hi, Keona. Hi, Sabrina," the girls said as they passed some of the housekeeping staff heading downstairs.

"Hi, girls," Keona and Sabrina greeted them cheerfully.

In front of Molly's door, the two friends waited until they were sure the coast was clear, then Molly whispered, "Let's see what's behind door number one!"

Laughing, they entered and looked around Molly's room, but nothing seemed to be new. Everything was familiar, cozy, and welcoming.

"Well," Molly said with a happy sigh, "they really don't need to bring something new every single day. It almost makes me feel guilty. I really have everything I need now, everything I could think of."

Except a mother or father—someone to love me, she couldn't help thinking. She pulled off her sneakers and wiggled her toes in relief, then put on her nice fuzzy slippers.

"Here's something," Evie said, picking up an envelope from the small folding table.

Curious, Molly raised her eyebrows at Evie, then opened it while Evie looked over her shoulder.

"Oh, my gosh," Molly breathed. Her wide green eyes met Evie's shining dark ones. "It's a gift certificate for The Gap! It's for clothes!"

"What?" Evie squealed, and she read the certificate herself.

"All right! That's a lot of money. You can get all kinds of stuff with that."

"I can't believe it," Molly said, holding the certificate as though it would disappear. "I'm so sick of looking awful. This is absolutely perfect."

"Wow. Your fairy godperson must be a mind reader," Evie agreed.

Molly looked up, a new light in her eyes. "I've got to thank them somehow," she said. "I don't want to find out who they are, but I've got to thank them—let them know how much it all means to me. When I think of how I would be doing right now without the magic . . ." She shuddered. "I know," she continued. "I'll write them a letter on my new stationery."

"That's a good idea. Then you can just leave it for them to find," Evie said.

"Okay," Molly said with a smile.

After Evie had gone to her own room, Molly took out a piece of the pretty stationery her mysterious friend had left, and sat down to write a letter. While her father had been alive, she had written letters to Brazil as often as she could. But this was her first attempt in over four months.

To my dear friend:

Every day I come back to my room and feel like I'm living a fairy tale. I can't tell you how awful things would be without your kindness. Knowing that you exist, and that you care about what happens to me, makes it easier for me to keep going. I don't know how I could possibly ever thank you enough.

And now you've given me this fabulous gift certificate. Ever since I lost all my clothes, I've been looking like the scarecrow from The Wizard of Oz. The kids in my class

101

say mean things sometimes. So having new clothes, and looking nice again, like a normal girl, means so much to me.

Ever since Christmas, I've felt so alone. But now I have so much: my friends Lucy and Evie, and you, and all your wonderful gifts to me, and my memories. No matter what happens this summer, I know I have those things.

I'm not trying to figure out who you are. I just wanted to say thank you a million times from the bottom of my heart. Thank you, thank you, thank you. I love you.

From the little blond girl in the attic.

It felt strange writing *I love you* to a complete stranger, but Molly really did feel as though she loved whoever had been so kind to her, whoever had saved her from that awful black hole she was in before the magic started.

She put the letter in an envelope, addressed it to her friend, and left it right on top of the folding table beneath the skylight.

"What a weird little girl," Leslie Banks mused as she read the letter on Friday afternoon. "What happened at Christmas, and how could anyone lose all of her clothes?"

Toby shrugged. "I don't know. But it's a nice letter. She's a nice kid. I wish we knew what her story is."

"Yeah." Leslie sighed and put down the letter. "I can't help wondering if this is how Molly Stewart has ended up. I mean, she's in some boarding school, but all of sudden she has no father, no one to pay the bills. What's happened to her? Is someone helping her? The whole thing just makes me nuts! Sometimes I can't sleep at night, wondering where in the world—literally—she is."

"You're doing all you can to find her," Toby said. "Mr. Price is tracking down every lead. I'm sure you'll find her soon. In the meantime, you can feel good about helping Anne."

"Yeah," Leslie said morosely. "It's not only that. I just have a lot on my plate right now. The lawyers are hashing out the distribution deal for *Fire in the Forest,* and I'm still waiting to hear from the New York Film Festival about eligibility."

"What are you going to do with the money from

Fire?" Toby asked. "You could start your own pro-
duction company, carry on Michael Stewart's work."
He gently kicked the tapestry chair he was sitting
in. "You could try to buy this house. It's a great
place for a movie company. Very classy."

A meow by his feet made them both laugh.

"Speaking of classy," Leslie said, leaning over to
pick up Mr. Tibbs. She cuddled the gray cat and
kissed his soft fur. "No, I don't know what I'm
going to do. Some of the money, what would have
been Michael's share, I'm putting into a trust fund."

"In case you ever find his daughter?"

"Yep. It looks like it's going to be quite a bundle,
if the movie does well. As for my share . . . well, I
don't know. I can't think about it right now." She
leaned back in her chair, settling Mr. Tibbs on her
lap. "I feel like I can't think about anything until I
find Molly Stewart."

"Well, since the movie is opening in New York
in three weeks, you'd better snap out of it," Toby
advised.

"You're right, you're right. I know you're right."
Leslie rubbed her head against Mr. Tibbs.

On Sunday afternoon Molly, Lucy, and Evie
were all miraculously free at the same time. They
threw on their jackets and raced out to the trolley stop that would take them downtown to
Faneuil Hall.

"We haven't been here in so long," Molly moaned as they walked around the shopping mall.

"There's The Gap. Let's go," said Lucy.

Three hours later, each girl carried a large shopping bag full of new clothes for Molly. There were jeans, T-shirts, sneakers, and practical tops, but also a few cute dresses and skirts and dressy outfits. She'd even had enough money to get new underwear and socks, as well as long johns and a warm hat for next winter. And she bought everything a size too big, so she could grow into it. She didn't know when she'd have another chance to buy new clothes. Her foster family might not want to spend money on her. A chill went down her spine whenever she thought of going to live with a bunch of strangers. They might be really mean, really awful. There was no way to tell. She just had to put it out of her mind until she absolutely had to deal with it.

"I hope the Thwacker won't be around when we get back," Lucy said as they slowly walked toward Glenmore from the trolley stop.

"Me too," Molly said fervently. She'd thought Ms. Thacker had been mean before, but the headmistress had really been on the warpath lately. When Molly had stapled some office papers together in the wrong order, Ms. Thacker had yelled at her in front of Susan and Mr. Thacker, and made her redo all of them. And a few days after that Molly had raced in to dinner after working in the garden, and she'd had dirt on her knees. Ms. Thacker had made her go upstairs to change into her only other pair of jeans. By the time she'd gotten downstairs again, all the desserts were gone. It made Molly feel constantly nervous, wondering what Ms. Thacker would do next. The only time she could really relax was in her own room at night.

Unfortunately, Ms. Thacker was in the main lobby, looking through her mail, when the three girls came in.

Smothering a groan, Molly tried to hide behind her bag and shuffle inconspicuously down the hall toward the doors of the girls' dorm. But no such luck.

"Miss Stewart."

Molly couldn't pretend she hadn't heard. Turning, she faced the headmistress calmly. "Yes, Ms. Thacker?"

"What are all these packages? Are they yours?" she asked Lucy.

"Well, no," Lucy admitted.

"Actually, they're mine," Molly said, deciding to just get it over with.

"Did you win the lottery?" The smile on Ms. Thacker's face was icy.

"No. I—I got a gift certificate." This was going to be hard to explain. Molly had really hoped to keep her secret friend secret.

"A gift certificate? From whom?"

"It was anonymous." Molly shrugged. "I found it . . . slipped under my door a few days ago. It was an envelope addressed to me, with a gift certificate for The Gap."

"Show it to me." Ms. Thacker's pretty face was tight-jawed and stiff.

Molly put her bag on the ground and fished out the letter.

It said: *For the little blond girl in the attic. Have fun buying yourself new clothes. From a friend.*

Ms. Thacker pursed her lips, then turned to Lucy. "Do you know anything about this?" Lucy shook her head. Ms. Thacker turned to Evie, but Evie was already shaking her head, too.

"I don't believe this," Ms. Thacker said stubbornly. "You will return all these clothes at once."

Molly's eyes widened. "I will not," she said calmly.

Ms. Thacker turned to Lucy and Evie. "Girls, you are dismissed. Molly and I will discuss this alone."

"I'm not going anywhere," Evie said grimly, crossing her arms over her chest.

"Me either." It was hard for Lucy's round, pretty face to look mean, but she tried.

"I don't know how you scammed someone into giving you those clothes," said Ms. Thacker, "but I intend to get to the bottom of this. For all I know, you stole them."

"I showed you the letter," Molly said, her finger-nails digging into her palms. "These clothes are mine, and I won't return them. You can't make me."

Ms. Thacker's jaw twitched, as though she was considering actually wrenching the bags away from the three girls.

"Fine," she said meanly. "But I *will* get to the bottom of this, and when I do, you're going to be sorry you ever tried to pull a fast one on me. Now get out of here."

The three girls turned and walked down the hall, through the double doors into the girls' dorm, and to the elevator. Molly was practically shaking with rage, and Lucy and Evie both looked furious, too.

In the elevator, Molly grumbled, "If it's anyone's fault I don't look respectable, it's hers. She's the one who sold all my nice clothes."

"I know," Lucy said angrily. "I hate her. Sometimes I just want to kick her in the shins."

Molly and Evie giggled at this image.

"It almost makes me glad I won't be here next year," Lucy continued as they got out on the fourth floor. "I'm glad you won't be here, either, Mol. No matter what your foster family is like, they can't be worse than *her*."

I really hope not, Molly thought.

"Was it her?" Leslie Banks leaned forward eagerly,

ignoring the huge pile of legal papers on her desk.

Mr. Price shook his head. "Nope. She was only about five years old, and her French mother was very much alive."

"But her name was Molly Stewart," Leslie protested, feeling frustrated and angry.

"No—it was *Marie* Stewart," Mr. Price explained gently. "Over the phone, and with a French accent, the names sounded a little similar. But didn't you say that Molly's mother is dead also?"

A pencil snapped in Leslie's hands, and she looked at it. "Yes. The Molly I'm looking for is an orphan. She has no one but me to take care of her, and yet I can't manage even to do that."

"What now?" The detective sighed. "Back to Europe? The Far East?"

"I don't know, I don't know," Leslie muttered, dropping her head into her hands. "Let me think about it. I feel so helpless."

Leslie was still lost in thought several minutes later when Toby came in with the mail.

"Yo," he said. "Registered letter. Looks like we're in the New York Film Festival!"

"Really?" Leslie almost smiled. "Great! I think the critics are going to love Michael's movie."

"It's your movie as much as his," Toby said loyally. "You did all the postproduction, and you put up a big chunk of money when he ran short."

"It was his idea, all his creativity," Leslie pointed

out, reading about their acceptance into the prestig-
ious film festival.

"Oh, by the way, I saw our little friend, Anne,"
Toby said with a grin. "Looking very spiffy, I
might add."

Leslie looked up, and her face softened. "Yeah?
She was wearing new clothes?"

Toby nodded. "She looks a thousand percent better. Her sleeves actually came down to her wrists,
and her jeans brushed the tops of her brand-new
sneakers. You did a good thing, Les."

"You're the one who's been risking your neck on
that roof," Leslie said. "I just put up the money."

"Not a lot of people would," Toby reminded her.

Leslie sighed. "It's the least I can do. I'm only
doing it because of everything I *can't* do for another
little girl."

"Look, all I'm saying is that apparently someone
cares about the child," Jerry Thacker said in his
mild voice. "Maybe we should tread a little more
carefully with her."

Ms. Thacker looked at her husband with dislike.
"You mean *I* should tread more carefully, don't you?
You think I'm too hard on her."

Mr. Thacker gave a little shrug and looked away.
Molly Stewart was a touchy subject with his wife.
He felt that she went too far sometimes—that she
was practically unreasonable when it came to Molly.

"You don't know how insolent she is to me," Cathy Thacker went on. "She's rude and snide, and she encourages her friends to be that way also. How can I run the school when I have this little traitor breeding trouble everywhere I turn?"

"She just doesn't seem that bad to me," Jerry said carefully. "I wonder if you're not, well, overreacting a little. In any case, someone gave her a gift certificate. We should be more careful."

Ms. Thacker turned cold, dark eyes on him. "Jerry, you just don't understand. That little princess has you wrapped around her finger. You just don't see her clearly, like I do. So butt out." Turning on her heel, she stalked out of the school office and slammed the door.

However, after the incident of Molly's new clothes, Molly thought that Ms. Thacker's attitude toward her changed a little. Maybe she was just looking forward to the summer, when she could dump Molly into foster care and wash her hands of her. Or maybe the fact that someone, somewhere, was interested in the charity student did make some sort of difference. At any rate, Ms. Thacker began ignoring Molly when she could, though she still assigned plenty of chores and office jobs. Sometimes, though, Molly would feel Ms. Thacker's eyes on her, and she would shiver with the cold dislike she knew was there.

But Molly tried not to let it bother her. These were the sweet days of spring, and her last month at Glenmore. What a year it had been! Her life had changed in so many ways. Soon she would be facing a really scary time—foster care—but for now she just tried to be as happy as she could.

Her new clothes were wonderful. They made her feel almost like a new person. She felt as if she stood out much less now, blended in more with the other students. When she'd first come to Glenmore, her fabulous designer outfits had made her stand out. Then, when she was wearing her oldest, raggedy things she stood out again, in a different way. Now she just looked normal, and it felt great.

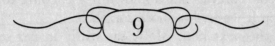

9

Mr. Tibbs Escapes Again

"Molly, please come here." Ms. Thacker stood in the doorway of her office.

Molly looked up in dread. It was Saturday morning, and she and Tran, one of the housekeepers, were rubbing lemon oil into the carved paneling in the main foyer. It had been several days since the headmistress had bothered Molly with a personal interview.

Inside Ms. Thacker's office, Molly saw Mr. Thacker, looking embarrassed and uncomfortable as usual, and a strange woman. Nervously fingering her gold locket, Molly sat down where Ms. Thacker indicated.

"Molly, this is Ms. Lindale. She's the social worker handling your case. We're here to go over some of the preliminary papers necessary for you to go into foster care."

Ms. Lindale turned and smiled at Molly, but Molly couldn't respond. Here it was. As much as she had put off thinking about it, it had still come. She really was going into foster care. She really was leaving

Glenmore, leaving Lucy and Evie, leaving Mr. Tibbs next door. Forever. She'd known it was going to happen. But it was still a shock somehow.

For the next hour Molly sat stiffly in her seat as the social worker explained everything carefully and slowly, as though Molly were stupid. Molly wasn't stupid. She was just numb.

At lunchtime Molly sat down alone—Lucy and Evie were nowhere to be found. When lunch was half over, Lucy finally burst in, grabbed her tray, and plopped down next to Molly.

"Where were you?" Molly asked.

"I was apartment hunting with Dad." Lucy's face looked rosy and happy, and she began eating enthusiastically.

"Really?" It cheered Molly up a little to see her friend so excited. "Did you find anything?"

Lucy shrugged. "We saw a couple of nice places. They were pretty and big, but of course it's not like having a real house with a yard and all. I think we may look again next weekend." She drank some of her milk. "It's weird—I've never really spent that much time alone with my dad before. During vacations Mom was always there, or he was working, and when I was little I had a nanny. But today it was just me and him."

"How was it? Did you get along?"

"Yeah." Lucy looked thoughtful. "Maybe it's better

now that I'm older and we can actually talk. He looks surprised when I tell him what I think about something. Maybe he just didn't know what to do with a little kid."

"It's great that you're getting along now," Molly said sincerely.

"So tell me about your morning, Cinderella," Lucy said with a grin.

Molly groaned. "Don't ask. I don't want to ruin your day."

"Well, go ahead and ruin mine," Evie said, setting down her tray with a bang. "It couldn't get much worse."

"This morning I met with a social worker," Molly said uncomfortably. "She was telling me all about foster care, and I had to sign a bunch of papers. The Thackers were there, too."

Lucy and Evie both looked at Molly in dismay.

"Oh, no," Lucy breathed. "Molly, I wonder if my dad would—"

"Don't you dare ask him," Molly cried. "He's going to have his hands full with you, and anyway, there's no way he would adopt a strange girl just to make you happy. No, it's pretty scary, but I just have to do it. After all, it won't be the worst thing I've been through." Her face softened. "Nothing could ever be that bad again."

Evie reached out and patted Molly's hand. "This really stinks," she said softly. "I just wish there was something someone could do."

"Anyway," said Molly, forcing a smile, "that was *my* morning. How about you?"

"Ugh. I saw my mom," Evie muttered, spearing a piece of macaroni.

"What's wrong with that? Is she still doing okay?" Lucy asked.

"Yeah. It's just—I don't know. She has this dream that everything's different now, that we can start over. She wants me to live with her this summer, and go to day school next year."

"Isn't that good?" Molly said.

"Not-really." Evie sighed. "It's just that I know nothing's really different. Sooner or later she's going to mess up again and go back to drinking, and then where will I be? I won't have Glenmore, or the Dukes, or you guys, or anything. All I'll have is her. And I can't trust her."

"You won't have us next year anyway," Lucy reminded her gently.

"Ugh," Evie repeated, her small, fine-boned face pinched in a scowl. "I don't want to talk about it."

Later that afternoon Molly was alone in her room. She'd told her friends she needed to start studying for finals, only ten days away, but she really just wanted to be alone with her thoughts. Now she lay on her thick, snuggly comforter and stared up at her ceiling.

Foster care. Evie had told Molly about it. She'd had some bad experiences in foster care. One family had

116

been really awful. The father drank, and when he was drunk he yelled at everyone, and the mother would lock him out of the house. One time the police had come. Another of her foster families had been really nice, wonderful people, Evie had said. She'd been so happy there. But then the father got transferred in his job, and they had to move, and they couldn't take Evie out of state. They'd tried to, and had even hired lawyers to figure out how to do it. But in the end they couldn't, and Evie had gotten sent somewhere else, while her family went away without her.

Molly drew in a shuddering sigh. She was really scared, she admitted to herself. She was only eleven years old—she'd have to be in foster care for the next seven years. Seven years was a very long time.

As she lay there on her bed she felt her nose start to get stuffy and her eyes start to sting. She knew she was on the verge of tears. *Oh, Daddy,* she thought miserably. *I guess you didn't know how bad it would be for me if you left me here alone. I bet if you had, you would have stayed, no matter what.* Of course, he hadn't had a choice. She knew that. But part of her still felt abandoned, lonely, lost. Afraid. Angry. At that moment even the happy thoughts of the magic didn't seem to help. The magic wouldn't follow her into foster care.

A tear slipped out of her eye and trailed sideways to her ear. She brushed it away with her hand. Then a scratching sound at her skylight made her sniffle and sit up.

117

Was it a bird, or a bunch of leaves blown by the wind? A shadow fell across the sunlit floor. Was it . . . it was Mr. Tibbs!

Leaping up, Molly ran to the skylight, feeling her spirits lift like a helium balloon. That's what she needed—a good cuddle session with the world's best cat. And there he was, pawing at the window. Molly quickly dragged her desk chair beneath the window and opened it. With a happy meow, Mr. Tibbs climbed onto her shoulder.

"Oh, sweetie," Molly murmured. "How did you know I needed you so much right now?" Holding Mr. Tibbs tightly, Molly got down from her chair and carried the cat over to her bed. He had grown even more since she had last seen him. Now he was an adult, with none of his kittenness left. Eight months before, when her father had bought Mr. Tibbs for her, he had been a tiny, blue-gray fuzzball. Now he was tall and sleek and full-bodied, with a grown-up cat face.

"You're still the most beautiful cat in the world," Molly told him, stroking his fur and scratching him under the chin. "I'm so glad they're taking good care of you." She kissed him, and he purred. "Oh, Tibbsey, what will I do when I can't even see you through a window? In just a few weeks, I'm leaving here for good. What if I never see you again?" To her dismay, she began weeping again, her tears falling on Mr. Tibbs. He purred louder and snuggled against her neck while she held him.

Time passed, and the afternoon sun began to slant through the skylight. Molly and Mr. Tibbs were curled up together on her bed. He was asleep, and she was almost asleep. Far away, she could hear a church bell chiming somewhere in the city. She knew it was time.

"Come on, sweetie," she told Mr. Tibbs, gently waking him up. "You know I have to take you back. But I promise to come see you at your house before I leave Glenmore for good, okay? I'll just ring the doorbell and say I have to see you. I bet Toby would let me. He's nice."

Molly buttoned up her new jean jacket, then stuffed Mr. Tibbs inside. He was a lot bigger than he'd been several months before, and her jacket was smaller and lighter than her old winter coat. If anyone saw her, she'd be sunk. Carefully Molly listened for footsteps, then tiptoed down all five flights of stairs to the side entrance. Just as she was sneaking down the hallway to the alley door, a voice said, "Hold on, Molly."

It was Julio, the kitchen assistant. Molly hardly ever saw him now that she no longer worked in the kitchen.

"Hi, Julio," Molly said quickly. "I'm in a hurry."

"What's that?" The young Hispanic man came over and looked at Molly's stomach curiously. "Molly, what are you doing?" he asked in a low, concerned voice.

Just then Mr. Tibbs pushed his head through the neck opening of Molly's jacket. Julio stared at him, then broke into a smile.

119

"I know that cat," he said softly. "It's Augustus's kitchen cat."

Molly smiled, remembering how the former cook, Augustus Bloch, had borrowed Mr. Tibbs sometimes so the cat could catch mice in the kitchen. "He lives next door now," she explained quickly. "I'm just taking him back. I have to hurry, before someone else sees."

Nodding, Julio went ahead of her to the alley door, and he opened it for her. He looked in both directions, then beckoned her through. Then Molly was in the narrow side alley that separated Glenmore from the stone townhouse next door. "Thanks," she whispered as she headed toward the street.

"No problem."

Once out of the alley, Molly turned left and went through the gate leading to the back door of Mr. Tibbs's house. She rang the doorbell. Mr. Tibbs was heavy and hot inside her jacket, and he was squirming restlessly.

"Hang on, sweetie," Molly muttered. "Won't be long now."

But no one answered the back door, and finally in desperation Molly carried Mr. Tibbs around the far corner to the townhouse's front door. She prayed someone would be home. There was no way she could hide Mr. Tibbs for much longer.

But Toby answered the door right away. He looked surprised to see Molly standing there with her jacket bulging out.

"I have your cat," she said shyly. "He came

through my skylight. I thought you might be worried about him."

"Come on in," Toby said, opening the door wider. "Actually, we've been so busy today we haven't even noticed the little rascal was missing. Here, come into the study. I want you to meet my boss. She'll want to thank you for bringing him back."

"Oh. Okay." Molly didn't know why she had to meet his boss, but she guessed it would be all right.

With one hand she unbuttoned her jacket, and Mr. Tibbs lay quietly in her arms. She cuddled him closer and kissed his head one last time between the ears.

"My cat seems to have developed an attachment to you," said a voice in back of Molly. Molly turned to see the attractive middle-aged lady she had seen once or twice before. Up close, Molly could see that she looked tired or worried, although she was smiling.

"Yes, well . . . I guess he was just exploring. Is it okay for me to put him down in here, with all the editing machines?"

"Sure, he plays on them any—" the woman began, then stopped. She looked at Molly curiously. "How did you know what these machines were?"

Gently Molly set Mr. Tibbs down on the Oriental rug, then rubbed her arms. He really had put on weight.

"Oh, I know all about editing machines," Molly said modestly, looking around. "My father made movies my whole life, until he died."

"Really," the woman said slowly. She seemed to peer

into Molly's eyes deeply, until Molly felt embarrassed.

"Well, I'd better go," she said, edging toward the door. The atmosphere in the room was suddenly strange—sort of quiet and expectant, and it made Molly uncomfortable.

"What kind of movies did your father make?" Toby asked softly.

Molly frowned. Why did he care? "Oh, you know. Comedies, dramas, documentaries. Everything, really. I used to go with him on location."

"Toby . . ." the woman said, still staring at Molly.

"Just relax, Les," Toby said quickly. He smiled at Molly reassuringly.

"What happened last Christmas, when you lost all your clothes?" the woman asked in a low voice.

Molly turned to meet her gaze. What a weird question. "My father died," she said. *How did they even know that anything happened last Christmas?* Molly wondered. At her feet, Mr. Tibbs twined between her legs, rubbing his head against her.

"Um," Toby said, "I know your name is Anne . . . but Anne what?"

Molly blushed at the mention of her fake name. But why were they being so strange?

"Actually," she said in embarrassment, "actually, it isn't Anne. I just . . . said that. 'Cause I didn't know you. I've been meaning to tell you. My name is really Molly. Molly Stewart," she said. "My father was Michael Stewart."

122

Molly Stewart, Found

The attractive middle-aged lady sank heavily into a tapestry chair. "Toby . . ." she said in a strained voice.

Is something wrong? Molly wondered. Maybe the woman had a weak heart or something.

"Your name is really Molly, and your father was Michael Stewart, the filmmaker," Toby said, watching Molly carefully.

"Do you think I'm making it up?" Molly asked, a little spark in her green eyes. This was all too weird. "Look. Here he is. This is my father." She reached up to her locket and snapped it open. Then she leaned forward to show Toby the two tiny pictures inside.

The woman, whom Toby had called Les, looked at them also. "That's him," she breathed. "And that's Marielle."

"How did you know my mother's name?" Molly asked in surprise. She'd died so long ago that few people knew about her.

"I knew her," the woman said, looking sad. "I

knew them both. Come and sit down, Molly, please. Forgive us for being so odd. But you see, I've been looking for you all over the world ever since your father died."

Molly stared at her. What was she talking about? There was a small stool in front of one of the editing machines, and Molly sat on it abruptly.

"My name is Leslie Banks," the woman said. "I taught your father in film school, many years ago. He was my most promising student. We stayed in touch, off and on, and I knew he'd married and had a little girl, and that Marielle had died. I even saw you once, when you were just a baby. Then Michael began making famous movies, and I was still teaching, and we lost touch for a while."

"You're his friend," Molly breathed, feeling as though the room around her was starting to swim. "He said an old friend of his was going to help him with the rain forest movie. You're her."

"That's right." Leslie nodded. "He contacted me, and the idea was so compelling that I took a leave of absence from teaching and flew down to Brazil. He was in a bad way—he needed more money, and I gave it to him. Then he got sick, and . . . anyway, right before he died, he asked me to take care of his little girl, Molly. I promised him I would." She lowered her head. "Before I knew it, he was gone."

Molly blinked hard, seeing Leslie's pain. It hurt, but in a good way, to see someone else who had cared about her father, who missed him.

"The movie was almost done," Leslie continued, "so I kept my rights in it, even after all the money vultures swooped down and broke up his film-production company."

Money vultures. Like Ms. Thacker.

"I knew you were in boarding school somewhere, but I had no idea where. I found nothing in his personal things that told me where you were. But I knew you were alone now, and I've been trying so hard to find you." Leslie's voice cracked, and she was silent for a moment. Molly couldn't think of anything to say.

"A private investigator has been looking for you everywhere for months," Leslie continued, "going to all these boarding schools, making phone calls, putting ads in papers all over the world."

"But I was right next door," Molly said slowly, feeling as if she were in the middle of one of her dreams. "Mr. Tibbs was my cat. Dad bought him for me. After he died, Ms. Thacker—she runs Glenmore—made me get rid of him. So I gave him to the old lady who lived here. And then you moved in and started taking care of him."

"Oh, Molly," Leslie said, her pale blue eyes gazing at her. "I can't imagine what it's been like for you for the last five months." She leaned forward and took one of Molly's hands in hers. "This seems like a miracle. Your dad was a very special person, and I loved him like a brother. But he never expected to die so young, and he made no provisions for you. I've been so worried, wondering who was taking care of you. I've been imagining all sorts of horrible things." Her voice broke again, and Molly could see tears in the corners of her eyes.

"All this time, someone was worried about me," Molly said in amazement. "Somebody cared." It was almost too much to believe.

"Yes, my dear," Leslie said. "I cared very much."

"Gosh," Toby suddenly broke in, after being quiet for a long time. "All this time I thought your name was Anne."

Molly blushed. "That was so stupid of me—but I was scared. I didn't know I could trust you. So I didn't tell you my name. I'm sorry."

"It's a good thing I didn't put 'To Anne' over all your stuff," Toby laughed. "You would have thought I was crazy."

"All my stuff?" Molly looked at him in confusion. "What stuff?"

"You know, all the stuff in the attic."

Molly stared first at Toby, then at Leslie. "All my presents? All my wonderful things?" she squeaked. "It was you who made the magic? You gave me everything?"

Leslie laughed and brushed away her tears. "Yes. It was Toby's idea, although we both had fun planning it. I was feeling so frantic over not finding Molly, and then Toby noticed how unhappy you looked. One night he followed Mr. Tibbs across the roof, and we were both shocked to see how you lived in that attic. So we came up with the anonymous-friend plan. Just to help another little girl, because I couldn't help my Molly."

"I had to move to the attic after Dad died," Molly said, her brain whirling to take all this in. "Ms. Thacker was so mad that I didn't have any money left. She let me stay at Glenmore as a charity student, but I work to contribute to the cost of keeping me. I've been so miserable since Dad died. When the magic started I felt like maybe I could somehow keep going. But . . . Ms. Thacker doesn't like me, and I'm going into foster care in two weeks."

"Foster care!" Leslie shook her head firmly. "Oh, no. We can't have that. Toby, please call the lawyers and see what we need to do."

With a cheerful salute, Toby left the room.

Turning to Molly, Leslie said, "I've been practically hysterical looking for you for five months. Now that I've found you, I'm not going to let you go. I have no children of my own. When Michael asked me to take care of you, it was like a dream come true. Suddenly I wanted a little girl more than anything. I couldn't wait to find you—all I wanted to do was to take care of you, and love you."

Sudden tears filled Molly's green eyes. It was like *her* dream come true, too. Looking into Leslie's face, Molly could see the kindness there, the caring behind the brisk efficiency. Could she really belong to this person, this friend of her father's? It was just so hard to absorb. This was who had created all the magic, who had saved Molly in her darkest hours.

"Really?" Molly asked timidly, wiping her eyes. This wasn't another fantasy, was it? Part of the magic? It was real, wasn't it? It would be so heavenly to belong to someone again.

"Really, my dear. Now I want you to tell me everything about the past year, ever since you started at Glenmore. And then what happened to you when Michael . . . when your dad died. I want to know everything about you, because you and I are going to be together for a long time."

And so Molly began, hesitantly at first, but then more confidently. Leslie was so warm and caring, and seemed so interested in everything that had happened to Molly. Molly sat next to Leslie on the couch, and they held hands. Mr. Tibbs curled up beside them, as if he couldn't bear to be left out. Molly felt as if she were finally eating a great big Thanksgiving dinner after going hungry for a long, long time.

Ms. Thacker looked at her watch. "It's dinnertime. Has Molly returned from her errands?"

Her assistant, Susan, shook her head. "Actually, Ms. Thacker, Molly never reported to me this afternoon for her errands."

"What?" Ms. Thacker's dark eyes blazed. So it

had come to this. Now that the child knew she was going into foster care, she wasn't even pretending to take her duties seriously. Well, Ms. Thacker would put an end to that, and pronto.

She stalked into the junior lounge and immediately saw Lucy Axminster.

"Lucy!" Ms. Thacker said, and Lucy jumped. "Where is Molly Stewart?"

"I don't know," Lucy said, a worried look on her face. "I haven't seen her all afternoon."

Tight-lipped with anger, Cathy Thacker began to search the other common rooms on the first floor. Molly Stewart was nowhere to be found. It was too much to bear. She was absolutely insufferable, and the sooner she was gone, the better.

"Excuse me, ma'am."

Ms. Thacker turned to see Mary, the head housekeeper, waiting for her. "Yes?"

"I heard you were lookin' for that Molly," said Mary. "I saw her myself, going into the house next door, about two hours ago."

"What? The house next door?"

Mary nodded.

Ms. Thacker turned on her heel and headed back through the main building to the front doors. The house next door? What did this mean? If that awful girl had forced herself on the people in the stone townhouse, Ms. Thacker would kill her, she really would. Molly Stewart had been nothing but trouble since the day she came, and it was time she started paying her dues.

"I just can't believe this is happening," Molly repeated, a look of wonder on her face. "And did you mean it . . . when you said I belong to you now?" It was hard to ask the question, but Molly felt so uncertain. It had been one of the strangest days of her life.

"I really meant it," Leslie said kindly, hugging Molly close. "Your dad asked me to, and I promised. He was very important to me, even though we lost touch for a few years. You have no one else. And you know what? I have no one else, either. So now we'll have each other. I'm sure I can adopt you, rather than let you go into foster care. I think it's what your father would have wanted."

For about the millionth time that day, Molly felt like crying, but these were tears of happiness.

Just then Leslie's young assistant knocked on the study door. "Excuse me, Ms. Banks. There's a lady here to see you. Says she's from the school next door." The assistant looked confused.

Leslie Banks stood tall, still holding Molly's hand. "Please show her in, Terri."

"It's Ms. Thacker," Molly whispered, feeling a trickle of fear run down her spine. "She's going to be mad." Was there some way the headmistress could stop this wonderful dream from coming true?

"Don't worry, Molly. I can handle her."

Ms. Thacker was shown in, and Leslie Banks released Molly's hand in order to shake Ms. Thacker's.

"Hi, I'm Cathy Thacker. I'm sorry to bother you," Ms. Thacker began with a pretty smile, "but I've come to collect a wayward student." She turned to Molly. "Please go home at once. I'll deal with you later." Giving Leslie a what-can-you-do shrug, she continued, "Some children are more difficult than others, I'm afraid. It's something I've learned, running a school."

"Molly will not be returning to Glenmore," Leslie said evenly, crossing to her desk and starting to stack papers neatly on it.

Nervously Molly looked at Ms. Thacker to see her reaction.

The headmistress looked dumbfounded. "Excuse me?"

Leslie looked up. "I said Molly will not be returning to your school. I wouldn't call it a home."

"But she must return there," Ms. Thacker said stupidly. "She's a charity student—she's under my custody. I'm sorry she forced herself on you this afternoon. I don't know what kind of incredible stories she's been telling you—"

"My assistant is currently on the phone with my lawyers and those of Molly's father, Michael Stewart," Leslie announced, coming back to stand beside Molly. "I imagine they can sort out the custody arrangement very quickly. And Molly did not have to tell me any stories; I know for myself what kind of conditions the child has been living in. I wonder what the parents of your other, more well-to-do pupils would think if they could see the attic where Molly has been living since her father died. And I wonder, Ms. Thacker, if you have ever heard of child-labor laws. I myself am in the film industry, and I know a great deal about child-labor laws. Our lawyers seem to think they're a very big deal indeed."

After this amazing speech, Ms. Thacker actually seemed to go pale. Her hands opened and clenched repeatedly at her sides, and her jaw worked without her saying anything.

Molly felt a small surge of triumph. If her dad were here, he would have said the exact same things; he would have stood up for her. Now Molly had Leslie to stand up for her, after so many months of trying to stand up for herself.

"Molly is an orphan," Cathy Thacker said finally. "A penniless orphan. Out of the goodness of my heart I took her in and allowed her to continue a very expensive education. I have clothed her and fed her, and received not one penny for it. I—"

"You must think I was born yesterday," Leslie Banks interrupted smoothly. "Molly may be an orphan, but she is far from penniless. Her father's last film is to be released in a week, and I expect it will make Molly a very rich girl. Not only that, but I'm sure when my lawyers, acting on Molly's behalf, examine your statements of account—and they will, I assure you—they will find that poor Michael paid for his daughter's tuition many times over. I knew him. It's the kind of thing he would do."

Molly sat on the couch breathlessly, watching this incredible interaction. To top everything off, Toby returned, looking confident.

"It's all settled," he said. "The lawyers seem to think there won't be any problem, especially after I described how Molly's been living for the last five months." He looked at Ms. Thacker. "You know, the attic, the raggedy clothes, the errands in snow-storms. That kind of thing."

A small choking sound came from Ms. Thacker's lips. Obviously the idea of Molly's having money again, and the threats of a lawsuit, were having an effect. Looking like a rat on a sinking ship, she turned to Molly.

"Molly," she said awkwardly, stretching her lips into a tight smile, "we've enjoyed having you at Glenmore, and I know your father thought Glenmore was the best place for you. If you return, you may have your old room back. And of course, there will be no more . . . work-study program. Will you do as your father would have wished, and return to live with your friends? I know Lucy and Evie would miss you very much if they never saw you again," she finished slyly.

"Of course she'll see her friends again," Leslie

said sharply. "Their parents aren't likely to refuse Molly's invitations. After all, once Michael's estate is completely settled, there are still his royalties from past movies, foreign rights deals, and so on. Molly will never have to worry about money again. I'm sure Lucy's and Evie's parents will be happy for their children to be friends with her."

Holding tightly to her gold locket, the one Ms. Thacker had wanted to sell with the rest of her things, Molly met the headmistress's eyes. Molly bit back all the things she longed to say to Ms. Thacker, all the things she had said in her dream. Instead she said only, "I want to stay here with Leslie. I won't go back to Glenmore. Not ever again."

Ms. Thacker's dark eyes almost bugged out of her head, and her lips thinned in the familiar, angry line. But Molly remained brave and calm. Ms. Thacker couldn't hurt her anymore.

Epilogue

Christmas in Boston

On a cold day in December, Cathy Thacker looked out her office window and saw a sight that she hated, one that never failed to irritate her completely.

A limousine was pulling up next door, at the stone townhouse. Three little girls—one blond, one dark, one with mousy brown hair—trooped out, their arms full of packages. They were laughing and teasing one another as they went up the townhouse stairs. None of them turned to look at Glenmore.

Ms. Thacker bit her lip so hard she almost drew blood.

"Oh, stop it, stop it," Lucy laughed, trying to pull some ribbon away from Mr. Tibbs, who was attacking it fiercely. "Molly, call him off! We'll never get our wrapping done."

"Come on, Tibbsey," Molly said firmly, scooping him up. She carried him over to the couch and plopped down with him on her lap. He immediately

135

curled into a big gray ball and closed his eyes.

"Not that he's spoiled or anything . . ." Evie said teasingly.

"I know, I know." Molly laughed. "But I'm so happy now, and have everything I want, and I want Mr. Tibbs to feel that way, too."

"I'm just guessing here," Lucy said dryly, "but I think he probably already feels that way."

"Pass the tape," Evie said, holding two pieces of wrapping paper together.

It was a few days before Christmas, and the girls had gotten together to do their Christmas shopping. Outside a light snow was starting to fall, but in the cozy study a fire was burning in the big marble fireplace.

"Hey, kids. Did you get everything you needed?" Leslie Banks stood in the open door, smiling.

"Uh-huh. I'm beat," Molly said, rubbing her cat behind the ears. "And I had to get a few things that Mr. Tibbs needed, too. 'Cause it's hard for him to shop. I think he might even have gotten *you* something, Aunt Leslie." Molly called her Aunt Leslie now, and she really did feel as though they were related by blood. In some ways, it felt as though they had been together forever. Since Leslie had decided to stay in Boston for a while to start on another project, it had made sense to stay in the stone townhouse. But they had gotten the attic window fixed so Mr. Tibbs couldn't escape anymore.

"Well, he's a thoughtful cat," Leslie said with a grin. "Do you girls want something to snack on while we wait for Lucy's dad and Evie's mom?"

"That would be great, Ms. Banks," Lucy said.

After she had gone, Molly looked at her friends. "Something tells me this Christmas is going to be better than last Christmas—for all of us," she said quietly.

"Yeah." Evie brushed her short dark hair off her face. "Of course, you'd be having a better Christmas even if you were about to crash in a 747. But Lucy's *definitely* having a better Christmas. And I guess mine will be okay."

"Yours will definitely be better," Lucy said pointedly. "I still think it's good for you to live with your mom, and you're only two blocks away from your grandmother. And your mom is doing really well. And you like your new school."

"Yeah, well." Evie busily applied herself to wrapping a present. "Anyway, my mother got a promotion," she muttered.

"Evie!" Molly cried. "That's fabulous! Tell her congratulations for me."

"Me too," Lucy said. "That's great."

"Yeah." Evie looked embarrassed. Molly knew she hated talking about her mother, even though they were getting along well and her mom was doing great. It would take a long time for Evie to relax about it. Maybe she never would.

In some ways, Molly felt the same way about Aunt Leslie. She was so happy living with her. The final adoption papers would go through next month, and Molly couldn't wait. But at the same time something inside her was scared it might not last. In November Aunt Leslie had gotten the flu, and Molly had been practically hysterical—she'd thought that maybe Aunt Leslie would die, just as her father had. But Molly figured she would get better about things like that as time went on.

"Well, *my* father has promised that we're not going anywhere for Christmas," Lucy said. "And no more of those awful family vacations to the Bahamas. We're just going to stay home and go to movies and stuff."

"When's your mom's wedding, again?" Molly asked.

"January." Lucy grinned. "They wanted to wait till the new year, for tax reasons."

"Your mom is such a romantic." Molly giggled.

"Uh-huh. The wedding's going to be so weird. I'm glad you guys are going with me."

"We'll protect you from your new stepsister," Evie promised.

Lucy's soon-to-be stepfather had one daughter who was in fifth grade. Next year she'd be going to Glenmore. But since Lucy was happy at St. George's, a day school, their paths probably wouldn't cross that much.

Leslie came in with a tray of drinks and cookies,

and she sat on the floor next to Lucy. Molly gently slid Mr. Tibbs onto the couch and sat on the floor next to Aunt Leslie. Mr. Tibbs didn't wake up.

"What are you working on now, Ms. Banks?" Evie asked politely. "Melina was asking me the other day." Melina and Philip Duke, Evie's patrons at Glenmore, had grown to care for her so much that they still did things with her, and gave her presents and kept in touch.

"I'm thinking about producing my own film," Leslie said, pouring herself a drink. "Since *Fire in the Forest* is still doing so well, there are lots of people who are willing to throw money at me." She smiled wryly, and shook her fine dark hair away from her face.

"Tell them what you heard, Aunt Leslie," Molly said.

Leslie grinned at her. "It's all very preliminary, of course, but we've heard rumors that *Fire in the Forest* will be nominated for several Academy Awards in February."

"That's great!" Lucy gasped.

Evie grinned and punched Molly lightly on the arm. "Way to go."

Molly smiled happily. "It's all thanks to Aunt Leslie. She's the best in the business. My dad always said so."

Suddenly Lucy raised her mug in a toast. "To the next year," she said, "and every year from now on.

Each Christmas we'll get together, and each Christmas we'll be happier. And we'll stay friends forever, no matter what."

"I'll drink to that," Evie said, clinking her mug against the others.

"Me too," Molly said, her eyes shining with happiness.

"Hear, hear," Leslie joined in.

On the couch, Mr. Tibbs opened his mouth in a wide yawn.